PRAISE FOR **DAIRY QUEEN**

2006 Borders Original Voices for Young Adults Award Winner
An ALA 2006 Best Book for Young Adults

"Delightful . . . a breath of fresh air . . . the sports scenes are lyrical. . . .The hilarious descriptions of D.J.'s family are a tonic for adolescent angst." —*New York Times Book Review*

"*Dairy Queen* is a wonderful first novel. . . . Not only is D.J. a highly likable character, her wry wit and humor make her a tomboy with heart and a great heroine for the YA genre." —*TeenReads.com*

"This bucolic first-person narrative also explores the emotional rollercoaster of first love in a funny, fast-paced, honest and poignant way." —*Chicago Sun-Times*

★ "A fresh teen voice, great football action and cows—this novel rocks." —*Kirkus Reviews*, starred review

"[Murdock's] first novel is the cream of the crop." —*Philadelphia Inquirer*

"This is a book that rings true and has heart to spare. Catherine Gilbert Murdock is a fresh and wonderful new voice." —Jennifer Holm, author of *Our Only May Amelia*

"I absolutely loved *Dairy Queen*. . . . It was funny and sad and I adored it." —Jaclyn Moriarty, author of *The Year of Secret Assignments*

"Eloquent and moving, and funny too. A small-town story about growing up one summer . . . and dragging your family along into growing up with you. Incredibly assured for a first novel." —Scott Westerfeld, author of *Peeps* and *Uglies*

"I loved this book." —E. Lockhart, author of *The Boyfriend List* and *Fly on the Wall*

DAIRY QUEEN

by

Catherine Gilbert Murdock

AN IMPRINT OF HOUGHTON MIFFLIN COMPANY

Boston

To James, and Liz, and Mr. Webster

All rights reserved. Published in the United States by Graphia, an imprint of
Houghton Mifflin Company, Boston, Massachusetts. Originally published in hardcover in the United States by Houghton Mifflin Company, Boston, in 2006.

For information about permission to reproduce selections from
this book, write to Permissions, Houghton Mifflin Company,
215 Park Avenue South, New York, New York 10003.

Graphia and the Graphia logo are registered trademarks
of Houghton Mifflin Company.

www.houghtonmifflinbooks.com

The text of this book is set in Dante.

Book design by Sheila Smallwood

Library of Congress Cataloging-in-Publication Data

Murdock, Catherine Gilbert.
Dairy queen : a novel / by Catherine Gilbert Murdock.
p. cm.
Summary: After spending her summer running the family farm
and training the quarterback for her school's rival football team,
sixteen-year-old D.J. decides to go out for the sport herself,
not anticipating the reactions of those around her.
ISBN 0-618-68307-0 (hardcover) ISBN 0-618-86335-4
[1. Football — Fiction. 2. Farm life — Fiction.]   I. Title.
PZ7.M9416Dai 2006   [Fic] — dc22   2005019077

HC ISBN-13: 978-0-618-68307-9
PA ISBN-13: 978-0-618-86335-8

Printed in the United States of America

QUM 10 9 8 7 6 5 4 3 2 1

CONTENTS

SCHWENK FARM

This whole enormous deal wouldn't have happened, none of it, if Dad hadn't messed up his hip moving the manure spreader. Some people laugh at that, like Brian did. The first time I said Manure Spreader he bent in half, he was laughing so hard. Which would have been hilariously funny except that it wasn't. I tried to explain how important a manure spreader is, but it only made him laugh harder, in this really obnoxious way he has sometimes, and besides, you're probably laughing now too. So what. I know where your milk comes from, and your hamburgers.

I'll always remember the day it all started because Joe Namath was so sick. Dad names all his cows after football players. It's pretty funny, actually, going to the 4-H fair, where they list the cows by farm and name. Right there next to "Happy Valley Buttercup" is "Schwenk Walter Payton," because none of my grandpas or great-grandpas could ever come up with a name for our place better than boring old "Schwenk Farm."

Joe Namath was the only one left from the year Dad named the cows after Jets players, which I guess is kind of fitting in a way, seeing how important the real Joe Namath was and all. Our Joe was eleven years old, which is ancient for a cow, but she was such a good milker and calver we couldn't help but keep her. These past few weeks, though, she'd really started failing, and on this morning she wasn't even at the gate with the other cows waiting for me, she was still lying down in the pasture, and I had to help her to stand up and everything, which is pretty hard because she weighs about a ton, and she was really limping going down to the barn, and her eyes were looking all tired.

I milked her first so she could lie down again, which she did right away. Then when milking was over I left her right where she was in the barn, and she didn't even look like she minded. Smut couldn't figure out what I was doing and she wouldn't come with me to take the cows back to pasture — she just stood there in the barn, chewing on her slimy old football and waiting for me to figure out I'd forgotten one of them. Finally she came, just so she could race me back home like she always does, and block me the way Win taught her. Smut was his dog, but now that he's not talking to Dad anymore, or to me, or ever coming home again it seems like, I guess now she's mine.

When I went in for breakfast Curtis was reading the sports section and eating something that looked kind of square and flat and black. Like roofing shingles. Curtis will eat anything because he's growing so much. Once he complained about burnt scrambled eggs, but other than that he just shovels it in. Which makes me look like I'm being all picky about stuff that, trust me, is pretty gross.

Dad handed me a plate and shuffled back to the stove with his walker. When things got really bad last winter with his hip and Mom working two jobs and me doing all the farm work because you can't milk thirty-two cows with a walker, Dad decided to chip in by taking over the kitchen. But he never said, "I'm going to start cooking" or "I'm not too good at this, how could I do it better?" or anything like that. He just started putting food in front of us and then yelling at us if we said anything, no matter how bad it looked. Like now.

"It's French toast," Dad said like it was totally obvious. He hadn't shaved in a while, I noticed, and his forehead was white the way it'll always be from all those years of wearing a feed cap while his chin and nose and neck were getting so tan.

I forced down a bite. It tasted kind of weird and familiar. "What's in here?"

"Cinnamon."

"Cinnamon? Where'd you get that idea?"

"The Food Channel." He said it really casual, like he didn't know what it meant.

Curtis and I looked at each other. Curtis doesn't laugh, really—he's the quietest one in the family, next to him I sound like Oprah Winfrey or something, he makes Mom cry sometimes he's so quiet—but he was grinning.

I tried to sound matter-of-fact, which was hard because I was just about dying inside: "How long you been watching the Food Channel, Dad?"

"You watch your mouth."

Curtis went back to his paper, but you could tell from his shoulders that he was still grinning.

I pushed the shingles around on my plate, wishing I didn't have to say this next thing. "Dad? Joe's looking real bad."

"How bad?"

"Bad," I said. Dad knew what I was talking about; he'd seen her yesterday. I hate it when he acts like I'm stupid.

We didn't say anything more. I sat there forcing down my shingles and doing the math in my head. I'd known Joe since I was four years old. That's more than three-quarters of my life, she'd been around. Heck, Curtis was only a baby when she was born. He couldn't even remember her not existing. Thinking stuff like that, there's really not much point to making conversation.

After breakfast me and Curtis disinfected all the milk equipment and worked on the barn the way we have to every day, cleaning out the calf pens and sweeping the aisles and shoveling all the poop into the gutter in the barn floor, then turning on the conveyer belt in the gutter to sweep it out to the manure cart so we can haul it away.

Back when Grandpa Warren was alive, the barn just shined it was so clean. He'd spread powdered lime on the floor every day to keep everything fresh, and wipe down the light bulbs and the big fans that brought fresh air in, and whitewash the walls every year. The walls hadn't been painted in a long time, though. I guess Dad was hurting too much these past few years to do any real cleaning, and I sure didn't have the time. So the barn looked pretty crappy, and smelled it too.

Whenever I passed by Joe Namath I'd take a minute to pat her and tell her what a good cow she was, because I had a pretty good idea what was coming. When I heard a truck pull into the yard, I knew it was the cattle dealer come to take her away. I gave her another pat. "I'll be right back," I said, like that would help, and went out to say hello at least. Delay it. Curtis followed me out because we don't get that many visitors.

It wasn't the cattle dealer standing there, though.

Dad came out of the kitchen pushing his walker, this satisfied look on his face. He spotted me. "I'm sure you know who this is?"

Yeah. I did. Curtis right behind me whistled between his teeth, only it wasn't whistling so much as blowing, like the sound bulls make when they're really mad. Because standing in front of his brand-new Cherokee in his brand-new work boots, looking about as much a part of our junky old farmyard as a UFO, was Brian Nelson.

2

PUT TO WORK

$\mathcal{L}$et me explain. See, Red Bend is my town and my school, and neither one is very big. There are about 130 kids in each grade—128 of us are starting eleventh grade next fall—and if you figure half of them are girls, and some of the skinny boys do cross-country, and some of the others have jobs or play club soccer, or I don't know, there's something wrong with them, that leaves about 20 guys to try out for the football team. Plus the other three classes, including the freshmen who are mostly still too little, and then you cut all the players who aren't any good, and the kids on JV, and you've got a team that's not the best there ever was, even with our league playing eight-on-eight instead of eleven players to a side like you see on TV.

Well, right next to us is Hawley, and Hawley has 200 kids in a class, which means that they've got almost twice as many guys to make up a football team. And for years, ever since these two towns were named, almost, Red Bend and Hawley have been enemies. Since they invented football back at Yale and Harvard, Red Bend and Hawley have been enemies. (I wrote a paper last year on how football was invented, which is why at least I didn't flunk history.) And Hawley almost always wins everything. That's why I was so mad about having to quit basketball last year, because us Red Bend She-Wolves had already beat the Hawley Tigresses once and we probably would have beat them again. But we lost, I mean our team lost, but I wasn't on it anymore—I was stuck working both milkings because Dad was so sick—and Red Bend lost in double overtime. That was the only time I ever saw Amber—my best friend—it was the only time I ever saw her cry.

Anyway, their football team is really good, and our football team is as good as it can be considering how small our school is, and the Hawley kids, and some Hawley grownups too, act like we stink and they're the best. Which isn't true. Four years ago when Win was a senior and Bill was a sophomore, Red Bend beat Hawley in the most completely amazing football game I have ever seen. My brother Win, even though he was quarterback and wasn't even supposed to be kicking, went in at the last second to attempt a field goal because this was his last game for Red Bend and he was just about the best player Red Bend has ever seen except for my other brother Bill, and he kicked it right through the goalposts like kicking a football was the only thing in life he'd ever done, and we won and, well, there isn't really any way I could describe what it was like, how everyone was screaming and my dad and mom were both crying and how Win was carried around by the whole team and then right there on everyone's shoulders he waved his hand up to the clouds because that's what we do to remember our Grandpa Warren who Win was named after, and then I started crying too, and it was — it was just a pretty amazing experience. Sometimes when I start thinking about how screwed up our family is, or when it's cold and I'm milking and the machines won't work and a cow steps on my foot and my hands are so cold I keep dropping things, then I remember how I felt at that moment and I feel a little better.

But most of the time when I think about Hawley all I feel is pissed off.

So when Brian Nelson stepped out of his fancy new truck in his fancy new work boots that his mother probably bought him at Wal-Mart, I was just about as angry as I've ever been. Brian Nelson's a Hawley quarterback. Hawley's backup quarterback, but still. Quarterbacks are always pretty full of themselves — even Win was sometimes, though he had a right to be — and Brian Nelson is just about the worst. He gets top grades and his father owns a dealership so of course he has a new Cherokee, and all the girls are after him, and last year he had scouts looking at him even though he wasn't a starter because his grades are so good that he'd raise the team GPA, which coaches always like. But ever since I've been watching him play, ever since junior high even, whenever he fumbles or messes up or gets intercepted, he always right off the bat blames someone else, which is really annoying to me and I bet it's even annoyinger to everyone else on his team who's working so hard. He's the very worst that a lazy, stuck-up, spoiled Hawley quarterback could be.

But there he stood in his fancy new work boots and his Hawley Football cutoffs and his Hawley Football T-shirt. "Hey, Mr. Schwenk, how's your hip doing?"

"Not too bad," said Dad, shaking his hand. "You know my daughter D.J., and my boy Curtis?"

"Hey." Brian nodded at us, and I could see just by the way he moved his head that he was thinking about all those games Hawley has won over the years and about how he had a new truck and new boots but we were just dumb farmers with a bunch of rusty old machinery and cow manure on our clothes who couldn't even pass sophomore English because we were so busy with farm work. Well, one of us was, anyway. Not that I thought Brian knew about *that*, but standing there I sure was aware that I'd gotten an F, right there on my year-end report card, and that he never would.

There was a really long silence.

Dad eyeballed me. "D.J., you gonna say hello?"

"No." That was great. Sometimes—well, all the time—I can't think of what to say because I'm so dumb and stuff, and then maybe I think of it like five days later. But I'll remember that one. For the rest of my life I'll remember that "no." Because if nothing else, it got a little bit of that smirk off Brian's face.

There was another long silence. If I had to make this into a movie, I'd have everyone count to twenty-five before saying anything. That's how long the silences were.

Brian cleared his throat. "Jimmy Ott thought I could, you know, help you guys out with haying."

"Jimmy Ott sent you over?" I asked, very suspicious.

He shrugged. "For the day."

Dad adjusted his walker. "D.J. here will put you to work."

Brian shrugged like it didn't matter to him one way or the other, and I shrugged the same way. But I wasn't quite so mad now that I knew Jimmy Ott had sent him over. I could put Brian to work. Heck, I could sure do that.

I jerked my head at Brian to follow me. "You know anything about tractors?"

Brian snorted like it was the dumbest question he'd ever heard. I knew he didn't.

"How about power takeoffs?"

He didn't even bother answering that one. Instead he just patted Smut, who ate it up, the traitor. "What's her name?" he asked.

"Smut."

"You're kidding. That's her name?"

I didn't bother answering.

For a while Brian stood there watching me hook the hay wagon to the tractor, but he wasn't helpful at all and besides, I was so busy showing off how good I was that I almost broke my thumb and then I had to pretend nothing was wrong, which wasn't so great for my mood. He ended up playing tug of war with Smut. Smut would play tug of war for two straight weeks until she collapsed of starvation and died. It really ticked me off that she was playing with him instead of staying next to me getting in my way and sticking her nose in my butt whenever I bent over. Not that I enjoyed that part, but she was my dog after all.

Right when I finished, the cattle dealer pulled in and I went to get Joe.

She was still lying in her stall right where I'd left her, chewing her cud with this really tired look on her face. I thought about the day she was born and how Grandpa Warren let me bottle-feed her for a couple days just because bottle-feeding is so much fun for little kids. I unhooked her, telling her how great she was and what a great milker she'd always been, and helped her stand up because her legs didn't work so good, and led her out to the yard one last time. There was no way in this universe I was going to let Brian Nelson of all people see me get all mushy over a cow. So I just handed her to the cattle dealer and he loaded her up in his wagon and off they went, Dad and I standing there to see her off.

Anyway, that was the last of Schwenk Joe Namath.

No one said anything for a bit except Brian, who was teasing Smut, trying to pull her rope away, not even interested in what just happened.

Dad glared at him. "What are you doing?"

"Uh, hanging out."

"Hanging out." Dad let those words rest in the yard for a bit. Hard to believe a guy with a walker could be so scary. "Hanging out, eh? You're here to learn how to goddam work, and if you want to start this season, you better get to it."

Brian stiffened. "Yes, sir," he said, not looking up.

In a way I was sort of sorry for Brian. I sure know what it's like to get both barrels. The only reason Dad got mad was because he was cut up about having to sell Joe. If this was a perfect world, we'd keep her forever and spend a million dollars trying to fix her sore legs and she'd die of old age in a rocking chair in some pretty green pasture. But this isn't a perfect world, it's Wisconsin, and feed costs money and vets cost money, and we barely have enough for the healthy cows, and the butcher pays us money for the old cows, and that money feeds the healthy ones. But of course Dad couldn't say that, any more than I could. I can barely figure it out to write it down. So instead he just beat up on Brian. Who deserved it.

Dad glared at me. "You got a job for him to do?"

I jumped. "Um, yeah. We're ready to go." I nodded at the tractor.

"Curtis!" Dad hollered.

As cut up as I was about Joe, I couldn't help noticing what Dad had said about how Brian needed to work for us if he wanted to be a starter. "Learn how to goddam work"—that's what Dad said, his exact words. I mean, it was one thing for Jimmy Ott to send Brian over because we were short-handed haying. But the fact that Brian had to come or he wouldn't get to play football, to *start*, which is a big deal especially if you want to play college ball, well, that was different. That explained why Brian even showed up at all. Because it wasn't like he was in love with us, or wanted to learn agricultural science. If he *had* to work for us, if it was some kind of test Jimmy Ott was giving him, well, that was something else altogether.

Jimmy Ott—I guess I should explain about him too—he's been the Hawley football coach for twenty-nine years. He sells insurance too, but mainly he's just a really good coach and a really good guy. A long time ago before Dad and Mom even met and even though Dad had played for Red Bend when he was in high school, Dad and Jimmy coached together. Dad had just gotten out of the army and he was living here with Grandpa Warren and Grandma Joyce, and the two of them ran the Hawley football program. That's how

Dad met Mom, because she was new in town teaching at Red Bend, and she went to the Red Bend–Hawley game because that's what everyone does, and they got to talking and then they got married. And even after they were married and living in the little house down by the highway and Win and Bill were born, Dad was still assistant coach. But then Grandma Joyce died and I was born and we had to move into this house and Dad had to quit coaching to work the farm, and they had to sell the little house off, and then Grandpa Warren died and Dad got the farm to himself and he doesn't coach anymore. But he and Jimmy Ott are still really good friends, and Jimmy Ott came to see him in the hospital, and he and Kathy Ott come for dinner a lot and they bring us Christmas presents because they don't have kids of their own.

When I was little it used to make me confused that we were rooting against Hawley even though Hawley was Jimmy Ott's team. I asked Mom about it once and she said it was because life isn't black and white, which didn't make any sense because Red Bend's colors are black and red, and Hawley's colors are black and orange. But later I learned what black and white meant and I thought I understood a little bit more, and then I just stopped thinking about it, which I guess is the same thing.

Anyway, Jimmy Ott used to watch us kids haying or milking or weeding the garden or playing a pickup game together and he'd just shake his head and say to Dad, "Boy oh boy, you sure did something right." Because us Schwenks aren't rich, and we're not that smart, and except for Bill, and Mom when she was thin back before she got married, we're nothing to look at. But one thing we can do is work. You want to learn how to work hard? Just look at us. We're about the very best place for a snotty, rich, sit-on-your-butt kid like Brian to go.

I began to realize, kind of excited, that if Brian had to help us in order to play football, well, that meant he'd have to put up with anything I dished out.

3

BRIAN BAILS

So off we went to hay, Brian and me and my chatterbox little brother. We rode up the hill, the tractor jerking along past cows grazing, past the timothy and corn and alfalfa.

"So, what's your workout schedule this summer?" I asked Brian all innocent-like.

He snorted.

"I'm serious. What are you doing?"

"It's vacation, remember? Summer vacation?"

"I'm just asking because Win and Bill worked out every day all summer. They'd do weights, stretches, pushups . . . Win even made a football field over there." I nodded at the heifer field, where the heifers spend all summer. If you don't know, heifers are cows that haven't been bred yet, haven't been married, as Grandpa Warren used to say. "My brothers would bring a couple of guys over and work out almost every afternoon."

"Jesus Christ," Brian said under his breath.

I ignored this. "You know, they say Win was just about the hardest-working football player Red Bend has ever seen. He was real talented, that's for sure, but he got that scholarship because he works so hard. He isn't that big either, but he gave every game and every practice two hundred and ten percent." I smiled at Brian. "You know, Win sure is one heck of a role model."

Just then we pulled into the hay meadow, the hay bales spread everywhere like trash after a party. I'd baled yesterday afternoon, and by now the dew had burned off so we could start bringing the bales in. It's really important that the hay be dry when you bring it in, because if there's any moisture it'll start to rot, and then heat up until the whole bale catches on fire and the barn burns down, which you don't want. Most of the farms around here use the new baling machines that make a huge round bale, so heavy you have to move it with a forklift. Knowing how poor we are, you're probably not surprised to hear that we have the same baler Grandpa Warren bought back in the Dark Ages, and it makes old-fashioned small bales that one person can pick up, more or less. You ever hear the term "backbreaking"? This job was about to define it.

"Can I drive the tractor?" Brian asked, trying to get out of the heavy lifting.

Curtis and I exchanged a look. Driving always goes to the weakest person. I started driving the tractor when I was six years old, when Bill who was nine could wrestle the bales into place.

I shrugged. "Sure."

Brian climbed in. "What's that pedal?"

"That's the clutch," I said.

"You mean this is a stick shift?" he asked.

"Yeah," I said, straight-faced. "No such thing as an automatic tractor."

Curtis snorted loudly. Brian flushed.

"Doesn't your dad"—I asked this as slow as I could, because it was, you know, worth lingering over—"doesn't your dad own a truck dealership?"

"We don't sell tractors," Brian said, like that explained everything. He was looking daggers at Curtis, who in his quiet way was rubbing it in. Curtis has always taken the Red Bend–Hawley thing really hard.

"Let's just have Curtis drive," I offered. We needed Brian, after all. Curtis and I could hay by ourselves if we had to— we had already done it twice this summer, but it had been pretty awful. So Curtis putt-putted back and forth across the field, trying to get as close to each bale as possible and slowing down when we were behind, while Brian and I humped bales into the wagon.

A hay bale weighs about fifty pounds and it's about the size of a filing cabinet, with two big loops of baling twine— rope, kind of—holding the hay together. That's how you pick up the bale, with the twine, and you'd better wear gloves because that twine will cut your hands up in about five seconds. Which it did to Brian, I saw, because he wouldn't wear them even though I said "There's gloves in the tractor" just as clear as daylight. It's hard enough to pick up a hay bale, but you sure can't toss one if your hands are all raw. So Brian would just carry a bale over and lay it in the wagon with this huge sigh, and then look at his hands, which were getting all pink, and then look down the field at all the hay bales we had left to get, and then sigh again like this was all too much.

Eventually at least he put the gloves on. He was smart enough to do that.

The thing with haying—or most jobs, really, that I know of—is that you can't think about how much you have left to do because that's just one thought, one sad thought, that'll make you bummed out all day long. Instead you've got to think about how much you've already done. I never look down the field, I just keep my eye on the wagon. First layer of bales in: hooray! Second layer: hooray! Third: yippee! And then the top layers when you have to really swing the bale to build up enough momentum to get it up there, that's even better, because it means the wagon's almost full and you can quit loading and drive back to the barn to unload. Although it's best not to think about that part either.

It was hard, though. I couldn't really get into a zone and just work away until it was done, because of Brian. Because every time he'd load a bale he'd wipe his face off and look at all the bales we had left and groan a little bit. Even though he was twice as slow as me. Really. I counted. I could easily get two bales loaded for every one of his. Plus he kept looking up at the sky too, like he couldn't believe that the sun was still up there burning so hot. But guess what: it was. Then he'd shake out his T-shirt, trying to lose the little bits of grass seed stuck all over his skin, but that's impossible to do once you're sweating. That's the thing about haying. It's hot and slow and backbreaking, but worst of all it's itchy.

So even though we were faster, kind of, than just me doing it with Curtis driving, it seemed a lot longer. And Brian couldn't figure out that hip thrust you need to get the bales up high, so he'd just hand them to me instead, and I'd toss them up and then climb up the side of the wagon to put them in place while he wiped his face off and shook out his T-shirt. Again.

"I really need some water," he mumbled.

"There's some back at the barn," I said.

He sighed.

We finally filled the wagon, and Curtis drove as carefully as he ever has back to the barn with Brian and me hanging on to the sides of the wagon, trying not think about how itchy we were. I was, anyway. I can't speak for Brian. Then I got to back the wagon up into the barn hayloft so we all could have so much fun unloading. It's not as much work as loading, thank God, because you don't have to walk as much. And you're out of the sun, although it's not like the hayloft is air-conditioned or anything. Or dust-free. Plus you have to be careful when you stack the hay bales because you're stacking them so high, and if you leave gaps the whole stack could collapse when you're climbing on it and break your leg. But at least Curtis was helping us unload, so we got it done faster. We didn't say too much.

Then, thank God, it was time for lunch.

We got to the kitchen and right there in the middle of the table were these huge, beautiful sandwiches with sliced tomatoes and everything, and pickles alongside. They looked like something from a magazine. I poked at them because I thought they weren't real, they were a joke.

"Wait till everyone's seated," Dad said for the millionth time.

Brian looked surprised as well. Surprised-impressed, not surprised-disgusted the way he normally looked. "Wow, Mr. Schwenk, those look great."

Dad shrugged like we ate like this every day. So that was it. Showing off for Hawley. I glanced at Curtis. He'd figured it out too, and he wasn't too pleased. If Brian wasn't there I would have asked Dad what TV show he'd seen them on, but instead I just started eating. It didn't make me very happy, though, Dad doing all this for a jerk like Brian. Something needed to be done about that.

"Brian," I asked, knowing the answer, "are you captain?"

"No."

Dad perked up a bit. "You're not captain?"

"No," Brian repeated, clearly just loving this topic.

Dad frowned. "You're quarterback and you're not captain? That's unnatural. If the QB isn't running the team, that's a team with a serious problem."

Brian just stared at his plate, chewing away.

We ate in silence for the rest of the meal, except that every once in a while Dad would say, just in case we hadn't heard, "QB has to be captain."

Dad and I don't get along most of the time. Maybe all of the time. But he sure did cooperate with me on that one, even if he didn't know he was doing it.

Heading back to the hay field for the second load, Brian didn't say too much, just studied his hands, which were all sore-looking. Welcome to farming, son.

"My brothers were both captains," I offered. "Win was captain even when he was a junior. He used to call everyone on the team every week all summer just to see how they were doing and make sure they were training enough."

"Jesus," Brian muttered. "If they're so perfect, how come they're not here?"

"Because," I chipped right in, happy I could brag about them some more, "they're both working at this football camp in Chicago with players from all over the country. There are scouts there and everything."

"And that's more important than helping your family?" Brian looked at me when he asked it too. Straight in the face.

I stared back at him, trying to think of some smart response, which was hard because all I could really think was that he'd just punched me right in the gut. That's how much that question hurt. And there was no way in heck I would ever tell Brian Nelson, of all people, why. But he just kept looking at me until finally I managed to get out something about how we needed to go to work, and we pulled into the hay field and started loading up the wagon, the sun beating down twice as hard while I tried to ignore what had just happened.

At one point, Smut, optimist that she is, showed up with her football, like we'd all stop working and play catch with her for a couple hours instead. And of course Brian did.

Okay. You've probably figured out by now that Brian Nelson is not my all-time favorite person. But I stood for a minute watching him throw, because he had just about the prettiest arm I'd ever seen. Even though Smut's football was a little flat and slimy, he'd just send it through the air every time like a bullet. And Smut would go tearing after it and bring it back just as fast as she could so she'd get to run after it again. Dang, he had a handsome arm. The rest of him was handsome too—which I'm sure makes you wonder why I haven't mentioned that before, but he was stuck-up enough already, and it didn't have anything to do with his arm anyway, as you would know if you thought about it for even a second. But still, I could see why Jimmy Ott would be interested in keeping this guy around.

Brian caught me looking at him and grinned like he'd won something, and I pointed to the wagon to remind him to get back to work, just to show I meant business.

So we finally filled the wagon, leaving half a load in the field that me and Mr. Cooperative would have to come back for by ourselves, because Curtis had to go to baseball practice. His Little League was almost to states, so it was a really big deal, and of course anyone on a winning team like that gets off chores. Brian was pleased to hear about that, you can be sure.

So Curtis went off with his ride to practice and Brian and I headed into the loft and started unloading. Brian every once in a while gave this little cough just to let me know how dry and dusty the barn was.

"Aren't you thirsty?" he asked after a while.

"No," I said, even though hay dust coated my mouth.

That made him mad, that I wouldn't get water and therefore he couldn't get water either because that would show what a wimp he was. His cell phone rang, one of those extremely annoying songs that cell phone owners are so in love with because for some reason they can't tolerate a plain old-fashioned ring. Finally whoever it was hung up and went back to painting her nails or something.

Brian kept sitting down. He'd lug a bale up the stack and then sit down on it, shaking out his arms each time like there was nothing in them. I've never seen anyone move as slow as Brian, not even Grandpa Warren with his arthritis. It was like he was in a contest to see who could do the least work, only he was the only contestant. Plus he was really angry now, which was good because it kept my mind off how thirsty I was. He muttered something under his breath.

"What?" I asked.

"You'd probably jump off the roof if they told you to."

"What are you talking about?"

"Don't you see how you live? You do all the work they expect you to do and you don't even mind. It's like you're a cow. And one day in about fifty years they're going to put you on a truck and take you away to die and you're not even going to mind that either." Brian shook his head like he was truly sorry.

"Oh yeah?" Which was a dumb response, I know. He was acting like he'd said something all deep and powerful, but if you haven't noticed, I'm not a cow like Joe Namath. I'm a girl.

"Forget it." He stood up. "I'm out of here."

"Why don't you get out your little cell phone and tell Jimmy Ott you're 'out of here'?"

Brian glared at me. "Screw you."

"Screw yourself. You stay here and work."

"This isn't work, what you do. It's stupid. It's stupid and pathetic and you can't even see it." He walked past me and right out the barn.

Through the grimy old windows in the loft I watched him stomp over to his Cherokee and really gingerly start the engine and drive off with just his fingertips on the steering wheel because his hands hurt so much. And you know, I felt bad. I really did. Because now I was stuck finishing up the haying all by myself.

Which I did, leaving the loaded wagon in the loft and taking our other even crappier hay wagon, and I had to keep jumping in and out of the tractor so I could load, and then leave that wagon in the hay loft too so I could go milk.

The good thing was that at dinner that night I got to tell Dad and Mom and Curtis all about Brian quitting, though I downplayed what a jerk Brian was because Mom always gets on our case for trash-talking other people. Dad still got really mad, though, and you could tell even Mom was upset about how Brian had walked out in the middle of a job like that. The two of them had one of those conversations with just their eyeballs, trying not to talk in front of us, and Dad called Jimmy Ott right after dinner, shutting the door behind him so we couldn't hear what he was saying. At least Mom made a big deal about me bringing in the rest of the hay by myself, saying over and over how great that was. That was okay, actually, getting all that praise and recognition finally, just because Brian bailed.

4

AMBER

Amber usually works Thursday nights, but this night she was off and I was completely psyched. Amber Schneider has been my best friend since forever, since I was in fifth grade and she was in sixth. Amber is really, really funny and really tough. I can look tough if people don't know me, but Amber just *is*. She's about the worst scorer on the basketball team and I don't think she could make a free throw to save her life, but she always started because her job was to guard the other team's top scorer, and she had this way of just really freaking out whoever that girl was, of messing with her, even though she almost never got called for a foul. I couldn't really say what she did but she would stare at them, and say things under her breath when the ref wasn't looking. Once a coach told her she had to work on anger management, but it seemed to me she was managing her anger just fine.

Plus Amber is big like me, which is nice. She told me once that I was built like a draft horse, which was a big compliment coming from her. Another time on a sleepover she did an imitation of me being carried across the threshold on my honeymoon, carrying me and everything, and I laughed so hard that pop came out my nose. That's why it's so much fun being her best friend, because I can be all goofy with her in a way I can't with anyone else.

She always wants to do my hair. She does stuff to her hair all the time, like during basketball season she dyed it fire-truck red to match our uniforms. It was—well, it was really red. She wanted to dye mine too but I wouldn't let her. This summer her hair was orange like a traffic cone. That's what it said on the bottle, even: "Traffic Cone Orange." Sort of to warn you how orange it'll be. Her mom Lori turned their living room into a beauty parlor and thinks she's some sort of expert, which she is if you're sixty years old, which I'm not. Sometimes when Amber is cutting my hair, Lori finds out and says *she* should cut it, and they get into a big fight with me sitting there under the sheet and everything, and the last time that happened, last year, I finally just said we had a cow about to calve even though that wasn't true and I left. And I haven't cut my hair since. Now I just wear it back in a rubber band and try not to think about it. It doesn't help that Win and Bill and Curtis all have blond hair, and Bill's is curly even, but mine is just plain old straight brown. I asked Mom about it once and she just shrugged and said that it just shows there's no justice in this world, which wasn't quite the volume of sympathy I was looking for.

✳ ✳ ✳

Anyway, that night Amber was in one great mood. She works at this restaurant that does fancy wedding receptions and stuff. She can tell stories about weddings that would make you never, ever want to get married, but she's so funny about it that it doesn't matter. For example, the wedding she was working had been canceled that morning when the bride caught her fiancé messing around with the maid of honor, who was of course the bride's best friend. Every wedding Amber works is like a soap opera. Anyway, the bride showed up to cancel the reception, and then the groom showed up after her to try to get her to change her mind, and then when that didn't work he tried to get his money back from the restaurant, and then the best friend showed up too, I guess because she's a total moron, and the three of them had a huge screaming fight right there in the restaurant kitchen while Amber memorized every word.

So you can imagine how completely happy Amber was to see me. She is one of those people who could describe tying her shoes in a way that would make you just about wet your pants, you'd be laughing so hard. So I was in a pretty good mood by the time we got to town, because even though my life pretty much sucks most of the time, at least I don't have my fiancé and my best friend trying to explain to me in the middle of a restaurant kitchen with everyone listening why it made perfect sense for them to be in the shower together covered in chocolate sauce. (I'm not so sure Amber didn't make up the chocolate sauce part, but she swears it's what she heard.) Plus she'd snagged a couple beers from her mom's fridge, and that was nice too.

The whole way into town when she wasn't telling me about Mr. Chocolate Sauce I told her about Brian, about how he was so lazy and stuck-up and how he quit right in the middle of haying, and she made me tell her over and over again about him getting covered in barn dust and hay, and how he picked up the hay bales like he was an old lady or something, and she'd laugh her head off each time she heard it. I was still feeling pretty good from all of Mom's praise, but that made me feel even better.

We went to the movies of course. I didn't have much money because I never do, but Amber never minds paying for my ticket or driving me around everywhere. The movie theater is about the only place in about three thousand miles to see a movie and it has eight screens, so that's where all the kids go, from Red Bend of course and Hawley and even places like Prophetstown and West Lake. The parking lot fills up really quickly, and sometimes the cops ask to see everyone's ticket to make sure they're not just hanging out, though I don't see why the owners complain because we're keeping them in business.

Amber found a place over in the shadows and we sat on her mom's Escort shooting the breeze. After a while Kari Jorgensen ambled over and joined us. She's going to be a senior like Amber and on the basketball team too, and I've always really liked her even though she's a little too popular for us. Amber told her about how the Hawley coach sent Brian Nelson over and he hadn't made it through the day before he quit because it was "so, so hard," and Kari got a kick out of that.

Just then a Jeep Cherokee pulled up under the very biggest light, music blasting away, and Brian and his Hawley football buddies and their skinny little girlfriends who are probably that type of vegetarian that doesn't even drink milk got out. Everyone else got quiet for a minute, which is obviously what Brian wanted or why else would he have parked there with his stereo going like that?

Amber said brightly, "They are so hot," which made us laugh.

So we sat there watching them in their letter jackets back-slap each other as their girlfriends giggled like there wasn't anything in the entire world these girls wanted to do except tell these guys how absolutely wonderful they were. It would have made me sick, except Amber was whispering to us her version of what they were saying. When Brian would punch someone in the arm she'd say, "I want your body, dude," like it was Brian saying it. Then she'd have the other guy say, "Oh, Brian, let me snuggle against you," and on and on until Kari and I were almost dying because we wanted to laugh so hard but we didn't want to miss anything she was saying. And then, as Brian had his arm around one of the prettiest, skinniest girls and Amber was saying (as Brian), "I knitted this sweater myself. See the neckline?" they saw us.

Actually, one of Brian's friends saw us first and pointed us out to Brian. Which meant Brian had told them about me. We certainly weren't the kind of girls they'd talk about or even say hello to if they could possibly avoid it. Pretty soon all the guys were elbowing Brian and laughing and pointing at us like we were some kind of freak show. Amber said, "They want to ask us out but they're too shy," which would have been funny except it was so obviously not the case. Then we could hear them making mooing sounds. I didn't like that one bit.

Then they started in: "There's Dairy Queen, Nelson! Go say hi to Dairy Queen!" The girls were laughing hysterically. And Brian was laughing too, looking over at me like I was the most disgusting thing in the entire world.

Amber stood up. "Let's kick his butt."

I pulled her back down. I would have loved to kick his butt, but we were outnumbered.

"What, like you're the only person here from a farm?" Kari asked. She's so great. That cheered me up more than anything.

Right then the cops showed up and everyone started going inside, including Brian and his moron friends, which didn't make me want to go inside too much.

Amber and I ended up behind the bank where her mom works. We do this a lot, which tells you something about how concerned the Red Bend police are with bank security. The one time we saw a cop, he parked at the other end of the lot and fell asleep. That night we started out like we always do, talking about how we'd rob the bank, which Amber is great at because she knows so much about bank security from Lori. Then Amber started complaining about how Lori wouldn't sign the permission slip so Amber could get a tattoo, saying Amber shouldn't do something at seventeen that she'd regret later. This is about the meanest thing I've ever heard anyone say, because Lori had Amber when she was seventeen so it's like Lori was saying that her having Amber was a big mistake. I was really beginning to regret that Amber had only snagged two beers when she started talking about all the people in Red Bend who are gay.

I know when you watch TV about half the characters are gay, and probably in New York or Los Angeles or someplace like that you could meet tons and tons of gay people, and I'm okay with that. Some folks around here say mean things, but, hey, as long as you drink your milk and don't call me Dairy Queen I don't care what you do. But I also know Wisconsin doesn't have any gay people. Or if it did, they all left.

But Amber could see gay people anywhere, from the high school principal (who combs his hair over his bald spot) to his secretary (who has big hands) through everyone, pointing out why each one was gay. It's especially funny because her examples are so good, like the kid who polishes his belt buckle or the basketball player who wipes his hands on his chest before each free throw. If I challenged her she'd just say that they were in the closet or in denial, which is something you can't really argue with even if you knew what it meant.

So she kept talking and then I kind of fell asleep, which isn't surprising considering how hard I'd worked all day, and Amber drove me home and I'm pretty sure I went to bed, but I don't even remember going up the stairs.

5

BACK TO NORMAL,
MORE OR LESS

*Y*ou'd think that someone who'd gotten up at five in the morning for the past six months would be pretty good at it by now. But Mom finally had to shake me awake because I didn't hear the alarm, and she gave me this look saying I shouldn't be out so late with Amber. She didn't say it out loud, but you could tell. When you teach school for as long as Mom has, you get those kinds of looks down cold.

The cows weren't much happier.

It didn't help that I couldn't stop thinking about Brian and his friends laughing at us. It was bad enough that we were from Red Bend and they were from Hawley. And that we didn't have any money and those guys were all loaded. Plus those stupid jokes I've heard a million times about how much farmers smell and how stupid they are, all those mooing noises. What really got me, though, was Brian's whole attitude, that working for us for even one day was the very worst sort of torture he could ever endure and only the threat of being benched would make him show up. Did our farm really suck that much?

And the problem was, I couldn't help feeling that it did. Those guys were class A-1 jerks, but the barn really did smell. This morning especially, and the flies were awful too, because I hadn't been doing so good a job cleaning up all the cow poop. And when I turned the big fans on, the fans that suck air through the barn to cool it off, they were so caked with cobwebs and crud that it's a miracle they even worked. There was so much dirt on the screens that even if the blades turned, they couldn't draw too well.

I hate it when people make fun of me and it turns out they're right.

When I came in for breakfast, Curtis had on his baseball uniform.

"Where's your game?" I asked.

"Eau Claire," he said, not looking up.

"Eau Claire?" I'd never played in Eau Claire. "You nervous?"

Curtis shrugged. He sure had a lot to say.

So they all piled into the Caravan—Mom and Curtis and Dad too, groaning about his hip like he was Joe Namath or something—and went to the game. It's been hard all these years for Dad to see our games with the milking schedule and all, but now that I was doing all the work he went to every single one.

Okay, I know that makes me sound like some kind of

slave, and I admit that right at that moment I sure *felt* like a slave. But before you call the cops to come and arrest him and Mom for child abuse, I should explain that it was partially my idea to take over all the farm work. I mean, it killed me having to quit basketball, and spend all spring knowing track was going on without me. But I started morning milking—well, after Mom asked me to—in January when it got to be too much for Dad to even get out of bed. And then in February, right before our second Hawley game, February 23, Dad came in for dinner just gray, puking almost, from trying to move the manure spreader, and it really scared me, the sight of him so shaky and weak. That night we decided that since Curtis was too young, and Win and Bill were away at college and had basically quit the family though no one mentioned that part, and we sure couldn't hire anyone to do the work, that it was going to have to be me. But let me tell you, I certainly didn't think when I took this on that Dad would take so long to get a new hip and I'd still be at it five months later.

So I sat there on the kitchen steps with Smut and my coffee, feeling really sorry for myself—a feeling I was pretty used to these days—and thinking about how I really needed to unload those two hay wagons. But I was about as interested in unloading that hay as I was in putting myself through the baler. Which, if you're wondering, is not very interested.

Instead I started looking around the farm like, well, like I was seeing it from snotty Brian's point of view. The house wasn't so bad—we'd gotten siding back when Grandpa Warren was still alive, it really just needed a wash. But the milk house and toolshed were all peeling paint. The granary, the old chicken coops we haven't used in years, the corncribs, all looked terrible. The basketball backboard was just a splintery old piece of plywood, the hoop all bent and rusty from when Bill thought he could dunk. Not to mention all the broken-down equipment we never moved, or the weeds growing everywhere like we don't care. Which we don't. It's not just that we didn't have the time for cleaning up, or the money. It's that no one wants to do it, at least not recently. We could have been a "Save the Family Farm" poster only it would have been too depressing.

So, right then and there, like a total moron, I decided to really clean out the barn.

Which was so *stupid*. I didn't want to clean it. I mean, I wanted to see it clean, but I didn't want to do it myself. I hadn't even finished unloading hay and we'd be haying clover soon, and timothy, not to mention silage in August, and just general farm work was enough, thank you, not to mention stuff like my life and that stupid English class that I couldn't even manage to pass.

But then all my anger at that stupid schoolwork I was going to have to do all over again, and Brian and his friends, and

Dad, and the state our family is in, got funneled somehow into cleaning. I dug through the toolshed, looking for supplies. I needed rags and brooms and stuff like that to get the dirt and gunk off the walls, and maybe a scraper; I wasn't really sure. Plus the toolshed looked like it had been in a tornado. Grandpa Warren used to keep the place spotless—you could perform brain surgery in there if you happened to need to perform brain surgery on a lawn mower. If he saw it now it would kill him, but then, he was already dead. Dad used to care, but he's been too hurt to care, and Win cared a bit until he went away, but Bill and Curtis . . . Someone needed to clean the toolshed too, but that wasn't going to be me. I knew that much. You had to know which little rusty screws to save and which ones to throw away, and I don't think even God knows that.

So I dug around and got pretty rusty myself, trying to find enough cleaning-up stuff. Then I went to work in the barn, fighting off flies everywhere, trying to get the ceiling dusted, all the dirty old cobwebs knocked down. I didn't do a very good job—mostly I just got dust all over me—but after a couple hours I could kind of tell where I'd worked and where I hadn't. Finally I got bummed out and quit, just as Mom called all excited to tell me that Curtis had won his game. Which was just extra superduper, because as long as Curtis kept winning, it meant he'd be at practice every day, and at games every week, and I'd be stuck working by myself.

That night at dinner I sat down starving, my hands all clean, and Dad handed me this big steaming bowl of puke. I'm sorry, but that's what I thought when I looked at it. Hot vomit. Curtis said grace—Mom gave him that job just to get him to say something but he's so quiet that I'm sure God can't hear him—and everyone else dug in: Dad because he made it, Mom because she's so happy not to be cooking herself, and Curtis as I said will eat anything.

I sat there trying to think of the best thing to say. What someone like Oprah Winfrey on TV would say to be polite. "So . . . what is this?"

Dad glared at me.

"It's good, honey." Mom smiled to Dad. "Very innovative." That's just the kind of word Mom would use too.

"It's just macaroni and cheese. With some other stuff mixed in."

I could see now. There were beans and hamburger and some green stuff, maybe peppers I think, all mixed together. It didn't taste all that bad, but I had to close my eyes to eat it, and breathe through my mouth too, because I was so sure it would smell like puke.

"You act like that, you can just eat outside," Dad said.

Oh, that made me mad. There was so much I wanted to say, about how I'd worked all morning on his stupid barn trying to make it look how Grandpa Warren kept it, how if he'd had his stupid operation back when the doctors said, he wouldn't still be in his walker with me flunking English and working like a slave. How if Win and Bill were around, if Dad hadn't started that huge fight that ruined our whole family, maybe none of this would be happening.

I think Dad kind of knew what I was thinking because he looked at me and held on to his fork like it was an ax handle. But no one said anything because, well, even when we fight we're not the world's best talkers. So I just shoveled that puke in and went to bed.

6

Jimmy Ott Steps In

Saturday morning, things were a little better. At breakfast I told Mom I was cleaning the barn and she told Dad, which is how Dad and I communicate most of the time because Mom actually likes talking to him, and a little while later Curtis showed up in the barn with this look like he knew I was about to put him to work. Which I did.

The day before with Brian, even when we hadn't been talking or when I was rubbing something in, I'd had the sense that talk was possible — if Brian, you know, changed into someone human. But with Curtis, no matter what you say you might as well be talking to yourself. Actually, talking to yourself is better, because at least you know you'll answer. Mom keeps getting Curtis tested to make sure there's nothing wrong with him, like his hearing or his mouth or anything. Or his brain. But the testing people just say that he's fine and he'll talk when he feels like talking.

Cleaning the barn with me, he didn't talk at all. It was like being with someone who does exactly as much as he needs to do to stay out of trouble. Which I guess pretty much describes Curtis to a T.

Luckily Jimmy and Kathy Ott came for lunch. I was really happy to see them, not just because it got me off work but because they're two of my favorite people. Jimmy's kind of short, and he's got red cheeks and this little belly that make him look like Santa Claus, but he's really fierce as a football coach. Hawley football is always really good, so I guess that Santa Claus fierceness pays off. Kathy's the only person in the world who still calls me Dorrie. Before I was born Mom wanted a girl so much she promised God she'd name me after both my grandmothers, which is why I'm stuck with Darlene Joyce which I totally hate. When I was little my family called me Dorrie until I switched to D.J. Kathy still uses Dorrie, though. Coming from her, it's like a reminder of the best parts of being little.

Anyway, she gave me a big hug even though I was all dusty, and Jimmy patted me on the back, and Dad came over with his walker and said I was doing a top-notch job cleaning the barn. Isn't that weird? Dad had all day to say that to me and he didn't. And then right when I was so busy being friendly that I didn't even have time to enjoy it, he jumps in. Maybe he thought I wouldn't notice. Or he was showing Jimmy what a great guy he was. In any case, the compliment was nice but it would've been nicer if I thought it was his idea.

For lunch Dad made chicken.

Mom couldn't have a garden this year what with Dad so hurt and her teaching sixth grade *plus* being acting principal at the elementary school because Mr. Ivanovich retired. And on top of that she had to spend all year going everywhere interviewing people to be the next principal, which no one wants because the pay's so little and who wants to work in Red Bend. So that's why they didn't have a garden, but Dad said not to worry because once everyone found out they'd dump their extra vegetables on us. Boy, was he ever right about that. Every day there was some more stuff left in the mailbox.

So we had zucchini with lunch too. Some recipe Dad made from you-know-where. With Parmesan cheese, like no one has ever eaten Parmesan cheese before.

Kathy couldn't get enough of it. "This zucchini is *so* good! Did you really make this?"

Mom smiled. "He's turning into quite a chef."

"This is the best zucchini I've ever tasted. I've got to get the recipe."

Which made Curtis and me bust a gut trying not to laugh at the idea of Dad writing one of those recipe cards.

Jimmy eyed me. "So, what'd you think of Brian there?"

Well. I buttered a roll and frowned, trying to look mature. "He's got a great arm. But I don't know how he'll handle the season." I took a little bite of roll because Mom gets on me about stuffing it all in my mouth at once. "He doesn't need a job so much as a personal trainer."

"You think so?" Jimmy asked.

"Oh, yeah," I answered, pleased that I could sound so grown-up when what I really wanted to say was that Brian wasn't worth a pound of salt and that Jimmy was crazy even to think about keeping such a stuck-up, lazy whiner on his team.

"I guess I was wrong, then, thinking he could help you folks out."

They all went back to talking about zucchini because I guess they hadn't discussed it enough the first time. But whenever I looked up for the next couple of minutes, Jimmy Ott would be sitting there studying me. It made me feel so weird that I stopped looking up and just plowed through my plate and ate all my zucchini without even realizing it.

After lunch and Kathy's amazing banana cream pie, Jimmy asked if he could see what I was working on. So he and I went out and walked around the barn, not saying anything, in this weird way I couldn't understand. He didn't even mention the wagons in the hayloft still full of hay because I hadn't unloaded them yet.

"You've taken on a lot here," he said finally.

"Yeah," I sighed, surveying the mess of the barn.

"I didn't mean the cleaning. I mean everything. Milking, field work . . . You're doing an awful lot."

I shrugged, getting all uncomfortable. It wasn't like I

deserved the compliments anyway, seeing as all I did was feel sorry for myself. "I've got Curtis."

"Your dad ran this farm with two boys plus you." Jimmy stepped over a cowpie we hadn't cleaned up.

I didn't know what to say, so I just rubbed at one of the windowpanes. Which was a mistake because it showed how dirty the windows were.

"I shouldn't have sent Brian over that way." Jimmy sighed. "I think you're right. You should train him."

"That's okay—What, me? His *trainer*? I didn't say I wanted to be his trainer!"

"You watched your two brothers train. You saw where it got them."

"Yeah, but—"

"You played Pee Wee football yourself. For four years if I remember it right."

"Only because Mom kicked us out! Dad had to take all of us on Saturdays—"

"You were pretty good."

"I was *nine*." I felt like I was in the middle of some practical joke. "Brian Nelson would rather chew glass than work with me."

Jimmy studied me. "I think you'd be a real good influence on him. And he could help out around here."

"He would never do it. Even if I wanted to," I added, just to make it clear that I didn't.

"My experience has been that an athlete will work for anyone he respects."

"Well, Brian Nelson doesn't respect me."

Jimmy polished his glasses. "Respect, D.J., is something
you earn."

Ouch. I didn't like that statement one bit. Jimmy seemed
to know more about Brian's haying experience than he was
letting on. "Okay," I sighed finally, just to say something. "I'll
think about it."

"That's all I ask, D.J." He patted me on the shoulder.

We strolled back to the house, not saying another word.

"You going to join us?" Mom asked from the porch, offering me an iced tea.

"I—I've got to check on some things," I said, heading off
to the barn.

"Dorrie is so responsible," I heard Kathy say. "You two are
blessed, you really are."

Then they were out of earshot, thank God, because I had
way too much to think about without adding anything more.

I sat in the equipment shed for about an hour, picking hayseeds off the baler, which of all the jobs on a farm is probably the very stupidest. Even sleeping is more useful.
Although, our baler's so old it should be in a museum. That
extra weight, those three or four ounces, probably isn't helping it any.

Why would Jimmy Ott say I could be a trainer? That was the craziest thing I'd ever heard. Although, well, I *could* be a trainer, and a pretty good one. I used to hang around Win and Bill all the time, watching them with their weights and their sprints and their drills. Win needed a receiver to catch his passes, and Bill being a linebacker needed a receiver so he could intercept those passes, so when we played together that's what I got to be, a receiver. I got pretty good at outrunning Bill, but I got even better at getting tackled because that happened a lot more often.

After Win went away to college, Bill still needed someone to practice with, so he'd get me to throw. The bad news is, I can't throw a football worth beans—I guess from all those years of basketball and volleyball. Most times it just ends up skittering off into nowhere. And every time this happened Bill would stop and look at me with this serious expression and say, "I thought you were a gifted athlete," because Mom made the mistake of repeating this once when she came back from parent-teacher conferences, and I'd chase after him trying to punch him and he'd laugh hysterically and hide behind Curtis, who'd be cracking up too. Luckily Curtis has a pretty good arm, so most of the time I got to be receiver instead and end up all black and blue from Bill's tackles.

Thinking about that made me really miss Bill. I wished I could talk to him. Find out what he was doing and stuff like that. But there was no way I was going to call him, and even if I did he'd probably hang up on me right away considering everything that's happened, which I'm not going to explain thank you very much. So I tried to stop thinking about him and think instead about what it would be like to train someone. Because it would be fun to work with someone like Kyle Jorgensen, who's QB for Red Bend this year. He's Kari's twin brother and just as nice as she is. I could think of a lot of stuff he and I could do together that would really help his game. Maybe coaching is just in my blood, from Dad and from Jimmy, who's as close to an uncle as I know, and from Win, who's going to end up coaching as sure as shooting.

After a while it was like those games I play with Amber where we talk about what we'd do with a million dollars. I was really liking the idea of being a trainer, in that way you like something while knowing it's never going to happen. Because even if I decided I could work with Brian, which I wouldn't, he wouldn't go for it in a million, billion years.

When I went back to the house, there was Jimmy leaning against their Explorer. He grinned at me. "You're interested. I can tell."

"Well, kind of. But I don't think it'll work out." Which was the most tactful way I could think of to express my feelings about Brian.

"You want me to ask your dad about it?"

"Don't you dare!"

Jimmy jumped a bit. "Okay then! I guess not."

"No, it's just—he'd want to get involved is all." Again, super tactful.

"Suit yourself. Kathy, you ready yet?"

Kathy came out with Dad's zucchini recipe and we said our goodbyes and they left. But the memory of them being here made the rest of the afternoon that much nicer.

Sitting here now, writing this all down, I'm beginning to see how Jimmy Ott might be a pretty good insurance salesman.

That evening at dinner when no one had said anything for a while, I screwed up my courage. "Dad, when you were coaching, did the kids, you know, respect you?"

Just as I thought he would, Dad made a crack. "Heck yeah, or I'd show them who was boss." He popped out his teeth and grinned at me. Dad lost a whole bunch of teeth playing football in the army, so he's got false ones now. When we were kids he'd take them out all the time and show us his big old toothless mouth. Curtis, the weirdo, used to love it.

"It's a good question," Mom said, of course. "Respect goes both ways, you know." She and Dad always double-team you on this stuff, backing each other up, I guess because they've been married so long.

"She's right," Dad added, scooping out some more leftovers. "You don't care for someone, they can tell."

"You cared for your players?" I asked, kind of incredulous.

"Of course I did! I was their coach."

"He bought us pizza," Curtis chimed in. When he says something, which is never, it's a big deal. Then he gets embarrassed because we all look at him.

Dad grinned. "It's true, I did. After every Pee Wee game." He looked so pleased that Curtis relaxed a bit. Curtis had officially been too young for Pee Wee football but they let him play anyway because he was so big, and because he was a Schwenk and all. Plus Dad was the coach and had to baby-sit Curtis whether he could play or not.

"You have to be fair," Mom said, "You can be firm—you should be. But the kids have to know you have their best interests at heart."

Dad nodded. "Winning helps too. But even if you don't win, you have to care."

In bed that night I thought over what Dad and Mom had said. I didn't care about Brian one bit. I made fun of him, I didn't make him wear gloves, I bragged all the time about my brothers, and I sure didn't buy him pizza. No wonder Brian didn't respect me. He might be lazy and spoiled and full of himself, but he wasn't stupid.

7

SUNDAY

Mom goes to church almost every Sunday. I used to go too when she made me, but one of the best things — actually, the only good thing when I think about it — about Dad's dumb hip was that I no longer had to. Milking fourteen times a week kind of got me out of that. Of course, since Dad slept in now and hobbled around complaining about how much he hurt, church was kind of an obvious activity for him. So he was stuck putting on his best shirt, which no longer fits because his gut's gotten so big, and groaning his way into the car, and riding off so the good Lord could mend his bones. His soul, I'm not so sure of. Not wanting to fight about it, Curtis had to go too.

I on the other hand, knowing there were three million jobs I should be doing, went back to bed, which was about the most satisfying thing I've ever done in my entire life.

Only instead of sleeping for three straight hours like I was hoping to, I woke up with a start only twenty minutes later when a blue Cherokee pulled into the yard. What the heck was Brian Nelson doing at our house on Sunday morning?

Not that I cared, because finding out would involve talking to him. Besides, he didn't come to the kitchen door or anything—just kind of snuck into the barn. If he was coming to steal something, the joke's on him—nothing to steal except cows, and he wouldn't put one of them in his Cherokee. But there was certainly a lot of stuff he could trash if he wanted to. Take our broken-down stuff and break it further. Or spray graffiti or something, graffiti about Red Bend.

So, pretty angry about having to get up, and even angrier about Brian, I pulled on a pair of jeans and boots and headed out.

Well, blow me down, as Grandpa Warren used to say. Because there was Brian Nelson in the hayloft, unloading the wagons. All by himself. With new gloves, I noticed, but still.

Now what was I supposed to do? I sure couldn't go back to bed. If nothing else, it would look pretty lame if he found out he was slaving away while D.J. Schwenk was napping. I could work cleaning the barn, but that would be a little weird, him in the hayloft while I scraped away below. The noise might freak him out or something. Besides, haying is hard work. You really need two people at least.

So in the end I angled my way into the loft and went to work emptying the second wagon. He looked surprised, embarrassed, actually, but he didn't say anything and neither did I. We worked in silence for a long time. Long enough that we were, you know, working together. That it was clear we were both doing the job.

"Hey," I said.

"Hey. I thought you'd all be at church."

So that was it. He showed up when he figured we wouldn't be here. That explained why he'd been working so fast and everything, trying to finish up before we got home. Only I already was.

We worked away for about twenty bales without saying anything more.

"Jimmy told me I had to do this," he explained, lugging a bale to the top of the stack. Which of course explained why he showed up at all.

"Oh."

We unloaded about ten more.

"You saw him?" I finally managed to ask.

"Yeah. He came by yesterday. Talked to me for a while."

"Yesterday afternoon?" I slid a bale up to him.

"Yeah."

"Did he, um . . . ?"

"Your big idea?" Brian eyed me kind of sideways.

"It wasn't my idea!"

"You mean you being my trainer and all?" Saying this, Brian's mouth sort of twitched.

"Can you believe it? That guy is totally insane!" I shook my head.

"Yeah, well, you should try having him as a coach." Brian wiped his face.

"Bill said he was real tough."

"Your brother said that?" He looked pleased.

We worked away for a long time. After a while I went inside and grabbed a couple pops and came back to the barn and tossed one to Brian. He caught it one-handed and nodded thanks. Then it hit me. A day before — even an hour before — I would have paid money to watch Brian Nelson perish of thirst. And here I was giving him a pop. Isn't that weird?

You should have seen their faces when Mom and Dad and Curtis came home. I can't blame them. Brian had made his feelings about us pretty well understood, and vice versa, and here we were three days later working together like it was the most natural thing in the world.

"Jimmy sent him over," I explained, like that made it all clear, and Dad eyeballed the haystack but I guess he thought better than to criticize it, and they went inside. Curtis kept looking back like he was worried about me.

We were just finishing up the last bales when this nice feeling spread through the barn, this really nice, hungry feeling, and it took me a while to figure out it wasn't a feeling but a smell: Dad was grilling. And all of a sudden I was so hungry I could barely stand up.

Mom appeared at the barn door. "Will you stay for lunch, Brian?"

Oh, jeez. Please say no. Please please please say no.

He shook his head. "I just want to finish this up."

"Oh, come on. Just one burger. We'd love your company." Mom beamed at him.

✳ ✳ ✳

Brian must have been starving because he ate that burger in about two bites, which was a mistake because Dad had made some fancy Texas barbecue sauce that almost took the roof of my mouth off. Curtis coughed so much Mom had to pound him on the back.

"Too much for you, huh? How do you like it there, Ryan?" Dad grinned.

"Oh, it's great. Sir," Brian answered, not correcting him on the name thing.

"Get you another one?"

"If there's enough, that would be great." God, he was playing Dad like a violin. "But I can, you know, put my own sauce on."

Even I had to laugh at that.

It wasn't that awful having him there. He and Dad talked about Jimmy Ott, and Mom asked him about his family, and when she found out he was an only child she said, "Isn't it nice you have football, then," in that really Mom way she has, but it didn't seem to bother him.

"Mr. Schwenk?" Brian asked, "why's your dog named Smut?"

Dad grinned. "You ever seen corn smut, son? It's a — what's that word again, D.J.?"

"Fungus," I muttered, my mouth full.

"Yeah, that corn gets. Turns the whole stalk black and powdery."

"You named your dog after a fungus?"

"D.J. did. It was her idea."

Brian glanced over at me but I just stared at my plate, wishing I weren't blushing. Finally, so he wouldn't think I was a total idiot, I explained, "Smut had this real soft black fur when she was a puppy and it reminded me of corn smut. That's all." I hated talking about it, and I knew Brian would make a crack. But when I finally got up the courage to look at him he was just smiling. Not smiling like I was an idiot, smiling like it was okay. That helped a bit.

After lunch Mom brought out the rest of Kathy Ott's banana cream pie. There wasn't too much left, and split five ways it wasn't much at all, but those three bites still made your mouth really happy.

So we were sitting there on the porch feeling pretty good, when Dad tossed a football to Brian. "Let's see what kind of arm you've got. Go on, you two, you catch for him."

Well, that was about the last thing I wanted to do, especially with Brian Nelson, especially especially with the last bit of banana cream pie still in my mouth making me happy. But you can't argue with Dad. So we hauled ourselves up, Brian looking even less excited than me and Curtis, and spread out on the front lawn.

"You want anything in particular?" Brian asked Dad, fishing for time.

"For you to throw the damn ball," Dad said so Mom shushed his language.

So Brian started tossing some passes with that really pretty arm he has. I could tell Curtis was impressed, and he had to really sprint at first, they were so long.

"Where the heck you think your receivers are?" Dad called from the porch, so Brian cooled it a little.

Actually, he didn't have the world's best aim. But it was fun running after them. Sometimes Curtis and I would go for the same ball and run interference on each other, the way we used to when Win and Bill were around. I love catching footballs. It's not like basketball where once you get the ball you have to immediately shoot or pass or something. With a football all you have to do is run, which is pretty great. Especially when you don't get tackled by your 230-pound brother Bill right afterward.

So it ended up being a lot of fun. We had a good time, Smut chasing us like she was on the team too. Once I caught the football and tossed it back to Brian, this pitiful wobbly pass, as awful as a pass could be, and Curtis paused and looked at me with this really serious expression. And I knew—I *knew*—that he was thinking that I was some kind of a gifted athlete, just the way Bill used to say it when the three of us would play together. And I took off after him like I used to chase Bill, and the way he ran showed me he really had been thinking it and I hadn't been wrong, and eventually I caught him because he was giggling so much, and I got him down on the ground even though he's half an inch taller now but still skinny yet, and I started beating on him and tickling him while he shrieked with laughter.

Brian and Mom and Dad stared at us like we were crazy. They didn't know the joke, and of course they hadn't heard Curtis say anything. But they were laughing too, just because it looked so funny.

After a while Brian looked at his watch and said he had to go, but he said it in a way that meant he really had to go, that he wasn't just trying to weasel out.

"I'm sorry, I didn't even ask." Mom frowned. "Your parents must be concerned."

"They don't care," Brian said flatly. "I just—I have to meet some friends." He tossed Curtis the football. "Thanks for the game."

I walked him back to the Cherokee because I owed him that much at least.

"That was fun." He sounded kind of surprised.

I wanted to say something about what it was like back when Win and Bill were around, but that was too painful. So instead I just said, "Yeah, it was fun." And then—I guess maybe because I was still feeling good from our game, or maybe just to clarify—I added, "You know, I really do know a lot about football."

"I know," Brian said. "Jimmy said so. He said you'd be a real good trainer."

My head came up. "You want to do it?" I couldn't believe it.

"No! I'm just saying . . . Why, do you?"

I studied my hands, all scratched up from haying. "Nah."

Brian picked at his steering wheel. "It's just . . . I need to get in shape. Jimmy said that with you beating up on me I probably could."

"Is that how Jimmy said it?"

"Well, yeah. You know Jimmy."

I thought about it. "I wouldn't beat you up that much."

Brian smiled at that. "So . . . you want to try it?"

"Maybe for like a week," I considered. Because he was just teasing me.

"Okay."

Which totally shocked me. "Okay then," I said back.

He cleared his throat. "But we don't have to, you know, tell anyone, do we?"

"Duh."

And he left.

Anyway, that's the story of how I became Brian Nelson's trainer. Which is the reason you're reading this. Well, one of the reasons, anyway.

8

PEOPLE WHO ARE CRAZY AND NEED TO
HAVE THEIR HEADS EXAMINED

If there was ever a TV show called *People Who Are Crazy and Need to Have Their Heads Examined*, I'd be the very first guest. They'd put me on one of those couches and a guy with a beard and funny accent would ask me questions, and the audience would ooh and aah as they realized this girl was crazy. What else would explain what I had just done? I've been thinking about it for months now, and I still don't have a good explanation. All I come back to whenever anyone asks me, including me, is that it sounded like fun. And — though it took Jimmy Ott to point this out — it was my idea. It's always a lot more fun to do something that's your idea. Plus Brian actually agreed to it, which still amazes me. I guess he decided that training with me for a week was better than benchwarming come September.

I know these aren't very good reasons, but they're all I can come up with. Maybe a shrink could figure out more if I had millions of dollars to spend on shrinks. But I do know this: I don't have many ideas, and not very many good ones. But this one got me excited.

And I stayed excited for the whole rest of the afternoon. During milking I thought about the lifts Win had used back when he was a high school QB, and how Brian could weight train in the barn while I worked. The free weights were still in the barn too, under a tarp. Mom wouldn't let Win and Bill keep them inside because their room is small enough as it is, and the two of them plus the weights would probably bring the house down. The weights were all dusty, but it's not like any football player ever said, Oh these are too dusty for me to train with. Thinking that gave me a grin. If Brian said anything, that's the crack I'd use on him.

At dinner Dad and Mom kept going on about how great Brian was, how hard he'd worked and on a Sunday too, how much he liked Dad's cooking, how nice he was, and on and on and on like he was the kid they should have had instead of us. If it had been one day earlier I probably would have barfed out of disgust. I mean, you could tell Brian was being nice just to impress them, and he was only doing the unloading to get in good with Jimmy. And sure he had an arm, but his aim stunk and he didn't have any wind or anything. You could see he was falling apart just by the end of our pickup game.

A couple times when Dad and Mom were laying it on extra thick Curtis caught my eye and I'd grin. But most of the time, because I was crazy, I sat there thinking about how I could build Brian's arm up, and his wind, and how his kissing up to Dad probably was a pretty good idea since we'd be sneaking around behind his back for the week because there was no way on this earth I was going to tell Dad what we were doing.

That night Amber called. "Hey, what'd you do today?"

"Nothing." On top of everything else, I'm a terrible liar.

"Liar!" Amber laughed. "Come on, tell me."

"Really. I milked the cows and took a nap." All of which was true, at least.

"What else?"

"Nothing. Really. What did you do?"

Eventually I got her talking about how much her job stinks, but I wasn't really listening. I hate keeping secrets, especially from Amber who hates it too—hates it when people keep secrets from her. But I sure didn't want her finding out about Brian, any more than I wanted Dad to.

And then all my enthusiasm faded away. What if Brian blew me off? What if he told his friends and they all made fun of me for thinking a dumb F-in-English farm girl could even be a football trainer? Because there's never been a teenage girl football trainer I've ever heard of. What if it turned out I couldn't do it? What if Brian did everything I said—which I didn't have too much faith in to begin with—but nothing happened, and Jimmy Ott said sorry but he'd made a mistake about me knowing football?

And what if it turned out just the opposite, that I was pretty good, and Brian stuck with it and people found out who turned Hawley's snotty, lazy QB into a real player? My folks would talk to me probably, but Curtis wouldn't. Amber would pretty much kill me, and so would everyone else in Red Bend, just for that one game if nothing else.

Let me tell you about that game, that one Hawley–Red Bend game two years ago.

Bill had trained all summer just to play Hawley. Every afternoon he'd go out to the heifer field and run his guts out, run until sweat poured off him like water, gasping Hawley's name every time he started his next sprint. He wanted to beat Hawley so bad—Win had beaten Hawley his senior year, and now it was Bill's senior year and everyone said he was even better than Win had been, bigger and faster and more versatile. By the time the game started Bill had worked himself up until he was in another place altogether.

Bill is a linebacker—someone who works defense behind the line of scrimmage, tackling runners, slowing down receivers. But that game Bill was everywhere. Every play he'd be somewhere else, up at the line or back, on either side of the field depending on where he thought the ball was going, ready to run down anyone, anyone at all from Hawley who came near him. Every time the Hawley QB reached for the snap, Bill would holler at the top of his lungs—we could hear it up in the stands; it gave me goose bumps—"That's my ball! I'm gonna get that ball!" And the QB—first their starter and then another guy, and then Brian, who was brought in at the end even though he was only a sophomore because the two other quarterbacks were so beat—would shiver a little, you could see it, and Hawley's offensive linemen would give this little twitch and step away from Bill without even realizing it. And not on that play, maybe, but within three or four plays Bill would run them down, get the ball somehow, get possession for Red Bend.

Then the Red Bend offense would screw it up. It wasn't like when Win was still playing when he was on offense and Bill was on defense and they balanced out. Instead, because our offense sucked so much, Hawley would get possession again and back in would go Red Bend defense, meaning Bill. That's what the game was: the entire Hawley team, eight at a time, against my brother. Hawley was ahead by seven for most of the game, and then in the last five minutes Bill intercepted a pass and ran for a touchdown, which would have been just fantastic except that the Red Bend kicker—I won't say his name because he's suffered enough—missed the extra point. And Hawley won.

And God, were they jerks about it.

Especially Brian. Every time he missed a pass or got tackled you could hear him chewing out the other Hawley players even though it was clear Bill would have wrestled a bear to stop the play. After the game, when Bill was crying he was so upset, Brian stood there in a crowd of Hawley players and jeered at him, calling him a baby and a girl and every name you could think of.

Remembering that game, well, you can imagine that didn't make me too pleased about Brian. He'd been fun this afternoon—that pickup game was okay, it really was. And he'd worked hard unloading the hay—worked like he should have worked three days ago, but still. And he was pretty civil to me, even. And that's what made me so confused. How could a guy who was such a jerk, how could he act so nice?

I was also thinking that if Bill ever found out I was training Brian Nelson, I wouldn't make it on to a TV show about crazy people. Because my brother would drive right up to Red Bend and kill me. You don't need to be speaking to someone to do that.

9

Dairy Queen

All through morning milking I tried to figure out how to get out of this mess. Me from Red Bend training Hawley's QB was a really bad idea, I could see now. I just had to figure out how to say it. I was still thinking about it, cleaning the barn, when Brian walked in.

"Hey." He was dressed in sneakers and everything, but he didn't look all too pleased.

"Hey," I said. I took a deep breath. "You know, we don't have to do this."

"I know. But Jimmy really wants it to happen."

"Oh." That sort of put a monkey wrench in my plans, knowing Jimmy was in on it.

"For a week," Brian added, just to clarify.

"A week," I agreed. So, not knowing what else to do, I showed him the free weights, waiting for his crack about the dust.

But all he said was "Jeez, I hate lifting," and started at least. After a couple minutes he sighed. "Win did this every day?"

"No." I wouldn't have said anything, but he brought it up. "Every other day. On off days he'd do sit-ups and jumps."

Brian gave me this really strange look. "Yeah. Of course he did."

I kept an eye on him while I scraped crud off the walls with a snow shovel. Once or twice I'd mention if I saw an elbow going out or his speed increasing or something, the way Win and Bill checked each other. I tried my very hardest to say it in a way Jimmy Ott would approve of, trying to earn Brian's respect and all. Not that I wanted his respect, but I owed that at least to Jimmy. Brian was okay about listening too, which I have to hand to him.

"You should power wash that," Brian offered once. "My dad has a power washer down at the showroom you could use."

"This is okay," I lied. I didn't know what a power washer was, and I sure wasn't going to ask. Instead I said, "When you're done there, we'll run some."

Well, "run" is an awfully flattering word for what we did. "Shuffle" is more appropriate. Because it was broiling already and it wasn't even noon. But at least we were moving forward, and breathing hard, though that was more from the heat than our pace. I knew if I didn't go with him he'd quit within a hundred yards, and then once I was with him I couldn't quit either, so we ended up running two whole miles without stopping. A couple times he tried to stop but

I'd tell him to keep going, mostly because I wanted it to be over so bad.

"You know," I said at one point, just to take my mind off how hot it was, "Bill ran this course every day his senior year."

I glanced at Brian. He looked furious.

We ran the rest of the way without saying a word. What a stupid thing for me to say, pointing out again how great my brothers were. So much for earning respect. This whole training idea was turning out to be too stupid for words.

We finally, after a hundred years, made it back to the farm. Brian climbed right into the Cherokee, slamming the door behind him.

I thought about asking if he was coming back but I was pretty sure what the answer would be.

"Wait," he said. He sat there picking at his steering wheel.

"You okay?" I asked finally because he wasn't saying anything.

"I . . . I'm sorry I was such a jerk at that game."

It took me a minute to figure out he was talking about Bill's football game.

"He worked real hard. He—Red Bend should have won." The words came out of him like they were being dragged, like it was ripping his guts out just to say them.

I swallowed. I hadn't been expecting this.

"And—I'm sorry those guys called you names last week.

And I'm real sorry I said that stuff about you being a cow, and dying and all."

"Oh," I said. "Um, thanks."

He started the Cherokee. "See you tomorrow."

Well, that gave me a little something to think about for the next couple hours. An apology? That was downright shocking. You could probably fill a book with all the stuff us Schwenks aren't good at, but what we're worst at is apologizing. Just ask Dad and my brothers if you've got the guts, because any one of them would smack you for bringing the subject up. Apologizing is like taking a little ache you feel inside and making it ten times worse. Like punching a bruise. Who'd want to go through that pain?

And you can see, just from Brian, why apologizing sucks so much. He was dying when he said it. Although he didn't look like he'd been all that thrilled beforehand, now that I thought about it. All that time I thought he was angry at me, because that's what you think if you see someone angry—it's what I think, anyway—but he was just angry with himself. That was interesting to think about too, the idea that you could be so mad at yourself that you'd need to apologize. Again, not something I've had much experience with. And you know, after he'd said all those things, banging away on his bruises, he still looked pretty cut up. But at least he didn't look mad anymore. I guess apologizing sort of released that.

But the more I thought about it, the more it seemed that he hadn't released all those bad feelings, he'd just passed them right to me. Because it hurt to hear him talk about what his friends had said, how they'd mooed and laughed at me and all. I'd forgotten how much I hadn't liked it until Brian brought it up. It shows why *not* to apologize: it just makes the other person feel bad. At least it made me feel bad.

Especially because then I started thinking about that last thing Brian had said, about me being a cow and all. I'd blown it off when he'd first said it when we were fighting. But now I tried to remember, because it obviously bugged him that he'd hurt my feelings. It took some time and some effort, but I did remember. And then I spent the next few weeks wishing that I hadn't. I wished it a lot. I still wish it sometimes, to this day.

Brian had said I was just like a cow, something about me dying—probably because he'd just seen Joe Namath go off to the slaughterhouse. He'd said I'd go up on a truck to die and I wouldn't even mind. Which was stupid, because people go in ambulances and die in hospitals like Grandpa Warren did. Besides, unlike cows I at least knew what I was doing. I mean, at least I got mad about stuff sometimes. I didn't much like getting up every morning, especially in the winter or when I was really tired, and I sure didn't like having to work every day with Dad breathing down my neck and treating me like an idiot.

Now that I thought about it, though, what good did it do

me, getting mad? Because I sure didn't tell Dad off—which he deserves—or quit. I just kept nodding even though I was about ready to kill him inside and went off to do exactly what he said. Which, I now remembered, Brian had also pointed out in his you-are-a-cow speech. That I did everything without complaining. Well, I was complaining inside, but who would know? My complaining inside just made me feel a little better. It kind of covered up—well, it had covered it up until now—how much I did what Dad wanted. Covered it up the way that frosting kind of covers up a bad cake, makes it go down easier. I just did what my parents told me, and my coaches, and Amber, and Smut, even. If Smut wanted to run back to the barn, I'd run even if I didn't feel like it, most of the time. I was nothing more than a cow on two legs.

Heck, maybe cows get mad too. I've seen cows get so mad they bust a fence or something, although that's rare. But maybe all day long they're seething inside and you just can't tell. They just keep getting milked and chewing their cud and having babies because they just don't know any different. Don't know any way to stop. Maybe they don't even like silage but they eat it anyway because that's all there is. I don't like Dad's food but I force it down or else I'd starve. If it was between that and starving, I'd probably eat silage for that matter, and act just like the cows do. I wouldn't get mad so anyone could see.

I sure didn't like thinking these thoughts, let me tell you. But every time I tried to stop they'd just come back into my head a different way, the way that Smut when you put her outside sometimes comes right back in through another door.

When I got in from evening milking Mom was at the kitchen table doing paperwork. After I'd eaten a bit and drunk about a gallon of milk, she looked up. "This afternoon I ran into Mary Stolze." Meaning the English teacher who flunked me.

I'd just been thinking that I couldn't possibly feel any worse and—BAM—now I did.

"She's real concerned about how you're going to manage this fall," Mom continued. "She still thinks you can finish some of the work you didn't turn in."

"So on top of everything else I'm doing, I've got to write a whole bunch of stupid papers?" I couldn't believe it. Those *stupid* English papers. Why of all nights did Mom have to bring them up now? Here I was trying to figure out what the whole point of my life was. The last thing I needed was to have to write a stupid paper on *Hamlet*.

"Honey, you won't be able to graduate without that class."

I kept eating, my head down. Mom kept talking but I didn't say anything else because that's what we Schwenks do. If there's a problem or something, instead of solving it or anything, we just stop talking. Just like cows.

10

WASH DAY

The fact is, I wasn't mad at Brian for what he'd said. It's like when someone breaks it to you that there's no such thing as Santa. It stinks, but hey, you've got to know sometime. You can't be thirty years old or something and still sitting up Christmas Eve waiting. You've got to learn sometime that the world sucks. And I'd just learned it.

Still, I sure wasn't interested in seeing Brian any time soon. But the next morning he pulled into the yard just as we were finishing our amazingly delicious burned pancakes and took this huge complicated thing out of the back of his Cherokee. So of course we had to go out and see what he was doing.

"That's a power washer," Dad said. I knew he wouldn't like it.

"I thought this might help with the barn cleaning," Brian explained. "Sir."

"Hmph. It makes a hell of a racket. D.J., you better move the calves outside."

Well. That was about the biggest shock of my life, Dad agreeing like that. So of course because I always do what

Dad says, I went and moved the calves out to the garden, which isn't a garden anymore but it's still fenced in, and Brian went to work with extension cords and hoses as Dad shuffled around with his walker, poking his nose into everything. Then, thank God, Dad and Curtis went off to Dad's physical therapy, because if Dad spent all morning nagging at Brian I would have died.

After his operation Dad of course couldn't drive, and Mom worked and even though I had a temp permit that let me drive him I had this little thing called a farm to work on, so it ended up that Curtis had to drive Dad around. At least Dad didn't beat up on him too much. That's one advantage to not talking. After a while people stop talking back.

I guess it was kind of a shock to Brian though, seeing that. His jaw just about hit the ground. "Your brother's like four-teen years old! What are they doing?"

"He turned thirteen last month." It was kind of fun, being matter-of-fact when Brian was so goggle-eyed. "They're just going to PT."

"But he doesn't even have a license!"

"It's a farm—he's driven for years. Besides, who's going to stop him? He's six feet tall."

"Jeez," Brian said under his breath. "Your family is so dif-ferent."

"Duh." I didn't say that to be funny or anything, I was just pointing out the obvious. But we both laughed anyway.

✳ ✳ ✳

Brian did a good job with the power washing; I have to give him that. He got all decked out in a raincoat and rain pants and big waterproof boots and went right to work spraying down the walls. It was like a fire hose just knocking all that dried-up gunk right off. In about ten seconds he got all the cobwebs and dirt off the windows better than I could have in an hour. Water sprayed everywhere, all over the ceiling and floor and his raincoat and the sawdust bedding in the stalls, which frankly needed to be replaced anyway. So I went to work shoveling all the bedding into the manure gutter, and running the gutter's conveyor belt to get all that waste into the manure cart, and basically doing the hard work while Brian just stood there like a kid with a new water gun.

"You want to try?" he yelled over the noise.

"I'd probably break it." Which I immediately regretted but it was too late because he shrugged and went back to his spraying. He even went at the big fans until they were brand-new clean, and I turned them on even though we might get electrocuted but we didn't, and they started drying everything out. And in a couple hours that barn looked better than it had in years. Except for the fact that most of the paint was gone now too, and in lots of spots you could see the actual stone from when the barn walls were built a million years ago by my great-great-grandfather.

Brian stripped off his raincoat, and it occurred to me that it wasn't just water soaking his T-shirt. He'd worked pretty hard. He packed the power washer back into his Cherokee while I drove the manure cart to the pit over the hill, little white paint chips floating on top. I sure hope that paint chips work as fertilizer because that's what they were about to become.

When I got back Brian was inside with Dad and Curtis, having lunch.

"What do you want to drink, son?" Dad asked him.

"We've got milk," I offered, which is a really old joke in our family because of course there's a 1,000-gallon tank in the milk house waiting for the milk tanker to come pick up the milk.

Brian cracked up, I guess because milk jokes were still kind of new for him.

Then I caught Curtis watching me. The expression on Curtis's face—well, he's the only person I joke with in the kitchen these days, and he didn't like me joking with someone else too much. And that one second of good mood I'd had laughing with Brian went right out the window. So we just ate. Brian said he could taste the horseradish in the sandwiches, which made Dad puff up like a rooster he was so pleased, but Curtis and I just stared at our food and forced it down.

After lunch Dad insisted on coming out to the barn with the new cane the PT lady had given him because he didn't need a walker anymore, which meant we moved about three feet an hour, and then once we got there you could see big puddles the fans hadn't dried out yet, and even though I figured Dad knew about canes and wet floors it still made me a little nervous. Not to mention him glaring at everything like this was a beauty contest or something.

"Needs paint" was all he said. Thank you too, Dad. He eyeballed Brian: "You know anything about painting, at least?"

"Um, what? I'm painting?" Brian looked blindsided.

"Jimmy Ott sent you over to work. Right, D.J.?"

God, Dad can be such a jerk. What was I supposed to say? That Brian didn't have to paint because he was only here for a week of preseason training? I'd cut off my arm before I said that. So I shrugged because I didn't know what else to do.

"Darn right," Dad added to himself. He inched his way back to the house, stomping that cane down each time like he was working a pile driver.

I turned to Brian. "You don't have to paint, you know."

"Aw, I probably should. If Jimmy Ott found out, I'd be in trouble with him all over again." He didn't look too happy about it, though.

I felt so bad that we messed around in the toolshed for a long time trying to find paint that was still, you know, liquid, and then because the barn was still too damp to paint we went running. It was cooler today at least, so it didn't feel so awful.

"I hope it's okay," Brian offered at one point, "me bringing the power washer over, after you told me not to and all."

"Sure. It was great."

"Jimmy said it would be okay. I was . . ." He grinned sheepishly. "I was complaining, you know, about how you wouldn't listen to anything I said about stuff like power washing. And Jimmy said not to take it personally because you didn't know anything about machinery less than forty years old. You probably didn't know what a power washer was."

I guess I could have gotten mad, but it was pretty funny. I grinned back.

Just then Mom passed us in her Caravan, looking a little surprised to see us out there on the road jogging away. I tried to figure out something to say about *that* but I couldn't come up with anything. Bringing up something stupid like the Vikings draft picks probably wouldn't work, seeing as Brian follows Green Bay. We couldn't really talk about training because it'd be like talking about breathing or something—we were already talking it to death. Maybe I could ask how truck sales were going? No, that would be the stupidest thing of all—

"You know," Brian said all of a sudden, spooking me, "I like running with you."

"Oh."

"When you don't feel like talking, you don't talk. That's pretty cool."

We ran the rest of the way without saying anything else, me wondering the whole time if he'd said that not talking in general was cool, or that I was.

✳ ✳ ✳

"So," Mom said at dinner in her fake casual way, "you're running with Brian?"

"Uh-huh." I polished off a couple pints of water.

"What's he doing running?" Mom asked.

"Training for football." Which was true.

"How come you're running with him?"

"Because he doesn't run fast enough." Which was also true.

"Well, that's awfully thoughtful of you," said Mom.

Whew. I didn't have to lie. I'm not too good at lying. And Mom, well, I don't know if she thought I was some kind of Good Samaritan or she was just too tired to bring it up, but she didn't mention that F or my English papers or anything like that. So that was good too.

I didn't realize until I was in bed that night that I hadn't thought one bit all day about being a cow, I guess because I'd been so busy. And I didn't think about it in bed either if you want to know the truth, because about three seconds after remembering the cow stuff I was asleep. You know that expression "fall asleep"? That's what it felt like. Like I was a plank that someone let go of and I just fell smack into this dark warm place where I didn't think or move all night, and that was just about the best thing ever.

11

Training

Brian and I sort of settled into a schedule. He'd show up after breakfast and head into the barn with me, doing weights
or sit-ups and jumps and stuff while I painted. Then he'd
paint too while we waited for Dad and Curtis to leave for PT
or food shopping or whatever, and then we'd really go to
work.

The problem was that the weather was too good. Every
day came up blue-sky sunny, and you could see on the
Weather Channel—which Dad keeps on all day because
weather's so important to farming—that it was going to be
blue-sky sunny for days. So because there wasn't any rain to
worry about, Dad announced on Wednesday morning that it
was time to mow the clover. Which meant *me* mow the
clover. Which meant me mowing and then kicking it the
next morning so the other side dries, and rolling it the *next*
morning so the dew burns off, and then baling and bringing
all the bales in just like hay. It was basically the rest of my
week. Super.

Coming back from mowing, though, I passed the heifer field and that gave me an idea, and then once I got to the yard that idea got even better because there was Curtis coming out of the house in his good shirt and everything to go to the dentist. He loves going to the dentist, which is the weirdest thing I've ever heard. We used to tease him all the time about it when we were kids. So he and Dad went off and I raced into the barn to find Brian rolling paint on the walls like he'd been stuck doing it for a million years, and I said, "Come on!" and off we went to visit the heifers.

The heifer field is about the prettiest spot on our whole farm. You can see for miles, the hills all patterned with hay and corn and pasture until they fade away into the sky. I climbed the fence and walked around, the heifers following me because they don't have anything else to do. I found that nice flat spot near the middle, and I stood there with my hands on my hips with the heifers all gathered around like they were waiting for me to make a speech.

Brian angled over, not all that comfortable around cows yet. Just because they're dumb doesn't make up for the fact that as heifers, or yearlings even, they're still pretty big.

"Yup. This is a field all right," he said.

"This is where Win and Bill used to practice. And me, when they couldn't get anyone else."

"This?" Brian was amazed. "But what about that . . . stuff?" Meaning the cowpies.

"Aw, jumping them teaches you footwork. You want to try it out?"

Trying to look all trainerlike, I whipped out the football I'd brought along. Brian looked like he didn't want to try it one teeny bit, but I guess he figured he didn't have much choice, seeing as it was this or painting. So he sighed and held out his hands, and I tossed it to him as best I could, and we started passing.

I made it really easy for him and stood in the middle of the field so he could work on his aim, which sucked. He'd throw the nicest little pass you've ever seen, and it would go sailing ten feet to my left and land with a little thunk and spook the heifers. Smut of course thought we were doing this all for her, and she was just about in heaven.

Every time Brian missed he'd blame something—the heifers or the wind or Smut distracting him.

"Stop it," I said. "That doesn't help."

"If it weren't for the stupid cow poop everywhere—"

"Ignore it. Just try again. And just—just concentrate."

It was hard. I've never been a coach before. You have to tell people what they're doing wrong without getting them all demoralized. I must have said ten times, "That was perfect. But try it this way . . ." It was extra hard because when I tried to point out his screwups he'd start complaining about why it wasn't his fault.

"So what!" I finally snapped. "You think there aren't distractions in a game?"

"This isn't a game. This is a cow field. In a game —"

"I've seen your games. You think your receivers like being chewed out for your mistakes?"

Brian tossed down the football and headed off the field.

I was happy to see him leave. What a whiner.

He was almost to the gate before I remembered that we only had three more days. Besides, he'd apologized to me on Monday, for something a lot worse than what I'd just said.

I took a deep breath. "Brian! I'm sorry."

He looked back at me.

"Come on. We promised Jimmy Ott a week. It's just until Friday."

"You know," he said, "it's not your job to bust me. It's your job to help."

I couldn't help grinning. "You mean Jimmy doesn't bust you?"

"Yeah! And do you see me standing out here with *him?*"

So we got back into a groove and he listened to me just a little bit more, a fraction of an inch more, when I told him he was standing wrong. Still, we got along okay. We kept saying "Just till Friday" whenever things got tense, like a little cheer almost. It made it bearable, knowing it wouldn't be forever, Brian so sore from all his weights and throwing and stuff, and me sore too from painting and our jogging in the afternoons, and both of us biting our tongues not to make a crack that would ruin everything. Just till Friday.

✳ ✳ ✳

Thursday Curtis had a baseball game, which was just as well.
He was supposed to help with the painting, only he worked
so slow and Brian worked so slow that watching the two of
them just about drove me insane. It wasn't like the slower
they went the sooner it would be done. There weren't any
painting fairies waiting to sneak in at night and finish it up for
them. The only one who'd be finishing it up was me. Which
explains why it made me so crazy. Plus Curtis was this big no-
talking presence, sucking away anything Brian and I might
have said. I got the sense that that sort of drove Brian crazy.
So as soon as Curtis and Dad left, we hightailed it up to the
heifer field to burn off some of our craziness.

"Okay," I said, trying to sound matter-of-fact, "let's start
with some sprints."

Brian stared at me. It wasn't a pretty stare.

I stuck a couple stakes at the other end of the field as he
poked at a cowpie with the toe of his shoe, just to make a
point. "You ready?" I asked in my best cheery voice. "Forty
yards. I'll run with you." I figured that would help him,
knowing we were both suffering.

So we lined up, Brian acting like this was his execution or
something—God that guy can bellyache—and off we went.

I'm a sprinter on the track team. My freshman year we
made regionals, we were so good. Of course I didn't run track
last spring because of Dad's hip. But now I remembered how

much I loved it, and how much fun it would be to run next spring.

"I think I'm going to puke," Brian managed to get out as we finished.

"Boy, that was great," I panted, wiping my forehead. "Want to do it again?"

He laughed.

"Come on, we only have four more." I headed back to our starting line.

Brian didn't move. "You're serious?"

"Yeah, why not? It'll be fun," I said.

Finally, just out of shame I guess, he shuffled over. "You Schwenks are insane. You hear me? Insane!" But I didn't hear anything else he said because I was already running.

Friday was my birthday. In the morning I celebrated by rolling and baling the clover, which was just amazingly wonderful, you can tell. Actually, it was better at least than having Brian find out it was my birthday. All that talk about how I wasn't sixteen yet—which is what a birthday means, it means you're finally turning an age that you want everyone to think you already are—I didn't want that talk at all.

Then Brian and Curtis and I had to go out in the afternoon to bring the clover in. At least I didn't have to worry about Curtis mentioning my you-know-what to Brian. If Curtis even knew it was my birthday to begin with. Anyway, the three of us got the wagon loaded, every last bale in that miserable sun, and unloaded the whole damn thing and collapsed on the hayloft floor because we were so beat. Working together like that, it sure was different from the last time we'd hayed. An awful lot had happened in one week.

Brian wiped his forehead. "I just hope come January that those cows thank me."

"I'll let you know," I said.

Curtis disappeared for a bit and came back with a couple big bottles of pop, which was about the best thing he's ever done in his entire life. We sat there passing the bottles around and belching. I'm not too good at it—I mean, I'm good for a girl and I can keep up with Amber, but that doesn't mean too much around here. Curtis is okay. Brian, though . . .

"Jeez," said Curtis, which is high praise coming from him.

So that was pretty fun, and we emptied both bottles and felt pretty good.

"You know," Brian said, "this has been the hardest week of my life. I don't know how you do it."

That was nice. We sat there for a few minutes, Curtis and me, savoring that. It was the very best present I got all day. Finally, though, I stood up. "It's been nice working with you."

Brian held out his hand. "Want to carry me to my car?" Which made us grin.

"Take care of yourself," I said.

"You too." And he drove away.

And that was the end of my big important week training Brian Nelson.

That night at dinner Mom and Curtis and Dad had a little birthday party for me. Amber had to work so she couldn't come, which was a bummer because she's always fun at parties. But Dad baked this cake that looked like a real birthday cake almost, and he gave me a jar of corn syrup as a huge joke on sweet sixteen. Curtis got me a Vikings jersey which was really nice of him because those things are expensive, and I guess it shows he knew it was my birthday all along. I can wear it around the house at least, because if I wore it to school I'd get beat up, all the other kids are such Packers fans. Teachers, too. Mom got me — ready for this? — school supplies. Thanks, Mom. Plus a card promising she'd take me for my driver's test ASAP.

That night I had a dream Dad was cooking up a big pot of hay, and we were sitting around the table eating it and we were cows. All of us. I woke up and heard the rain starting, and you'd think I'd get some satisfaction from bringing all the clover in safely. But I didn't. Instead I lay there trying to figure out why I'd wanted so much to turn sixteen years old when now that I actually was sixteen I didn't feel one little bit different.

12

THE LONG WEEKEND

I've got to hand it to her: Mom lived up to her promise. Saturday morning right after milking she drove me to the Department of Transportation so I could get a driver's license. Well, not a real driver's license because this is Wisconsin, where they treat teen drivers like they're insane homicidal morons, but at least a probationary license that lets me drive *by myself* so I don't have to beg Mom and Amber for rides anymore.

Don't even ask what my photo looks like.

So because it was still pouring rain and I couldn't do any farm work, thank God, I drove the pickup *by myself* to Amber's, where we watched *Blue Crush* for the millionth time. It's a movie about three girls who are a lot like us except they live in Hawaii and don't have any parents and they date professional football players and surf all the time. And they're thin. So you can see that the similarities are overwhelming. Also Amber got me a really great box of chocolates that we gobbled down in about fifteen seconds. And because I was so sore from haying, she gave me a really great shoulder rub until she poked me in the ribs and I cracked up.

"You know," she said, "I'm thinking about working checkout at the Super Saver. You should too—they've got openings."

I tried to figure out how to respond. I didn't want to say it, but something about those checkout people has always made me really uncomfortable. It isn't just that they have to stand in one place all day and make small talk—both of which I hate—and call to ask the price of stuff—which I could never do—and remember all those numbers—which I would stink at. Thinking about it, I realized that they were cows too. Just like me. That's what they reminded me of: cows standing there in their milking stalls all day long, waiting to be milked. Although of course the checkout ladies don't get milked. But cows at least get to go outside occasionally, which the checkout ladies never do unless they're going for a cigarette, which isn't the same thing.

So I said, trying to be all tactful, "I've got farm work."

"Oh please. You're not even getting paid."

"Yeah . . . but what about volleyball?"

"Volleyball sucks." Which is true.

"It'll suck even more if you're not there."

"So work with me. We'll buy that F-150 together." Amber is saving for a pickup.

"Yeah, but . . . but don't checkout ladies remind you of

cows?" It was a little awkward bringing it up, but I figured it would at least give us a chance to talk about it.

"Cows?" Amber looked at me. "What are you talking about?"

"Well, you know, the way they just stand there?"

Amber patted me. "Girl, you need to get off the farm. Want some popcorn?"

So she popped a bag and we hung out for a while more, but it wasn't the same. I could tell she really wanted me to take that job. Comparing her future coworkers to large domesticated animals wasn't winning me any favors. And to tell you the truth, I was a little mad too. I'd really hoped we could, you know, talk about this whole I-am-a-cow thing. I was as pushy as I know how to be, but she sure didn't have any interest.

So I drove home all by myself in the rain, thinking how nice it was not to have to ask Amber for a ride because I sure didn't feel like asking her for anything at the moment. I did the evening milking with thirty-two wet, smelly cows steaming up our new clean barn, and went to bed early because there's never anything on TV and I wasn't in the mood to go out.

I lay in bed thinking about working checkout at the Super Saver and how I would rather die than get a job like that. Beyond the fact that I hated the idea of it, I wouldn't be any good at it. Which sort of brought up the issue of what exactly

I would be good at. Certainly nothing that involved talking or working with people, which crossed a whole bunch of jobs right off the list. Kari Jorgensen for example works at her folks' ice cream parlor. That would kill me, having to deal with kids, and talk to people all day long about which flavor tastes best. It's ice cream. It doesn't matter. It's good. All of it. Trust me.

About the only thing I was really good at was farming, but I sure didn't want to spend my life doing that. The one other thing that came to mind was football. It was a shame Brian and I only had a week. Maybe after I got out of high school, if I ever got out, I could hang around and help out Red Bend's football team like the old guys who showed up sometimes to be line coach or something. Maybe, that is, if I were a guy.

Maybe I could join the circus. Ha. I'd seen carnivals at the county fairs where kids show their animals and they judge the best watermelon and all that. The folks who worked the carnivals always looked like they were having about as much fun as the checkout ladies. But maybe a circus was different. Maybe I could clean up after the elephants. I sure knew a lot about that. And in the end that's what put me to sleep, thinking about elephant poop.

The next morning as everyone except me was getting ready for church, Mom said for the millionth time, "The front lawn needs cutting."

"I thought we'd just hay it," I said. It's an old, old joke in our family. No one laughs.

Mom sighed. "I'm just hoping it can get mowed before it looks any worse." That hung there in the kitchen for a while. You could hear Dad thinking that his hip was still mending and Curtis thinking he had baseball and me thinking that since I do every other damn thing around here, maybe someone could take the tiniest bit of responsibility and do it themselves.

Then they left and I paced around the house, too wound up to sleep and too bored to do anything normal like watch TV or something. Or read. We're not big readers in this family. *Farm Journal* maybe, or *Good Housekeeping*. Or schoolbooks when we have to. But you can bet money I wasn't too interested in those. Finally, so I wouldn't go insane, I cranked up Grandpa Warren's old ride-on lawn mower and went to work on the lawn.

It wasn't much fun, let me tell you. The mowing was fine—I could mow that lawn in my sleep, especially since we've basically given up on flowers and stuff. But it sure didn't make my brain any happier. There wasn't much that made my brain happier these days. The only time I really enjoyed myself, it seemed, or I was too busy to realize I *wasn't* enjoying myself, was with Brian. Even painting or haying was okay when he was around because we were so busy. But training was the best. Planning it, doing drills with him, timing his sprints on our so-called football field . . . That field could be a lot better. Cleaning up the cowpies would be a start. Mowing down the humps of grass the old cowpies had turned into. Once all those were gone I could get some lime even, and mark out the lines . . .

So after a while, without even doing the sides of the driveway and all the other stuff, I went back to the toolshed for a measuring tape and lime and stakes and the line marker Win made out of a baby stroller and a coffee can, all there in a pile from when he and Bill left them because no one ever cleans up anything ever, and made myself a couple peanut butter sandwiches and headed up the hill.

I worked right up until milking time even though there was so much other farm stuff to do that was more important. Although now that I think about it, I was doing it *because* there was so much other stuff to do that was so important. But this was fun. It was my hobby. The way Mom does needlework sometimes even though, let's face it, how many little scratchy pillows does one family really need.

Anyway, it was great. I scooped up all the cowpies and dumped them in a pile. I mowed the whole football field and marked all the lines as straight as an arrow, more or less. The heifers were interested for a while but then they just chewed their cud and watched me like I was a TV rerun they'd already seen. They didn't like the lawn tractor too much, but I hoped the memory of all that racket would keep them off my field.

It was about the prettiest football field you ever saw. Well, half a field. I only went to the fifty-yard line because even half a field is a lot of work. The grass was bright green from all the rain, and the white lines were clear as a bell, and the contrast between the long heifer grass and the freshly mowed field made it look that much better. I kind of wished I had a hot air balloon or something to take a picture. A little voice inside me asked just what exactly I planned to with this nice new field, but I smashed that thought right down. If that thought had been a fly, I would have killed it with a fly swatter.

During milking I looked once or twice down to the end of the barn where the weights were, almost like I expected to see Brian there. Which is crazy, I know. Like how Smut sits next to the kitchen cabinet waiting to be fed when we've already fed her. Crazy, but you can't help hoping. Then, when I couldn't put it off any longer, I went into the kitchen prepared for the worst. Frankly, I was surprised Dad hadn't already bawled me out for not finishing the front lawn. Him not showing up meant he was extra mad, sitting at the kitchen table just steaming.

When I came in, though, he and Mom barely looked up. "You've been busy there" was all Mom said.

"How about this one?" Dad asked her, holding up the Betty Crocker cookbook.

"I'd stay away from marshmallows," she answered.

"What are you doing?" I had to ask.

Mom sighed. "At church your father got in a fight with Connie Ingalls—"

"A discussion," Dad interrupted. "They were *dry.*"

"You hurt her feelings, you know," Mom said.

"I didn't *say* they were dry. I just said—"

"Anyway, Dad said that I could make better brownies and he'd prove it." She and Dad had clearly been through this a couple times.

"But you never make brownies."

"I'll make them," Dad said like it was obvious.

"You'll make brownies for Mom?" I was confused.

"Your mom's too busy."

"But—if you're making them, then they're *your* brownies."

"Men don't make brownies," he sniffed. "How do you feel about chocolate chips?"

I looked at him sitting elbow-deep in cookbooks, recipe cards everywhere, a jar of corn syrup—my corn syrup, my birthday corn syrup—right in front of him. "Whatever," I said, and went upstairs to take a shower.

Curtis was at a sleepover so I couldn't even joke with him about Dad. I couldn't really talk to Amber about it. She and Dad don't get along too good in the best of circumstances. She'd make some crack about how you don't need boobs to make brownies, which is true but still. It's one thing to call your own father a moron but it's different when someone else does it. And with Amber not having a dad and all, it was even harder. Because I couldn't point out her own father's mistakes except for that one about him leaving before she was born, and that I wouldn't do.

You know who I really wanted to talk to about the brownie thing? Brian. Because he'd find something to joke about, some way that was funny but not mean so even Dad would laugh. And thinking about that made me really miss Brian. Because, well, maybe you haven't figured this out yet, but I don't have a whole lot of people in my life to talk to, and Brian was someone I could. Even when we didn't talk, which was most of the time, I felt okay with him. And then I started thinking about his training and how the worst part was over, and how if he kept it up it would only get better and he wouldn't be so sore. Plus it would really impress Jimmy Ott that he'd decided to keep going.

And then right away before I changed my mind I dried off and went into Mom and Dad's room where the phone is and closed the door so no one could hear me because that would be the worst, and I looked up Nelson in the phone book and they were listed, thank God, because I didn't have a solution if they weren't, and called him.

The phone rang four times. One more ring, I decided, and I'd hang up.

"Hello?" a woman answered.

"Yeah—hi." I swallowed. "Is, um, Brian there?"

"Brian!" she called. "There's a girl on the phone for you!"

I blushed deep red. Okay, I know I'm a girl and that I was calling him, but I wasn't *that kind* of girl. He must get a hundred calls a day from girls. They sure called his cell phone enough. I should have called his cell phone—then I wouldn't be interrupting his mom. But I didn't even have that number. And if I did call it, that would make me seem even more like a girl on the phone—

"Hello?" Brian said.

"Hey. It's, um, D.J."

"Hey, how are you?" At least he didn't sound angry.

"Okay." I tried to think of something to say, but all I could think of were all those girls who called him and how they probably were much, much better at this.

The minutes ticked by.

"You want to put Curtis on, let him talk for a while?" Brian asked.

I cracked up, because I was so nervous but also because it was funny. And then, all at once so I wouldn't stop myself, "Last week was real hard but it's going to get easier so maybe if you wanted we could keep going with the whole training thing."

"Huh," said Brian as I tried to breathe. "You know, you're right. It would get a lot easier with the base I've got. It's a real good idea."

I nodded. Which was stupid, seeing as he couldn't see me.

"But you know, I just got this lifeguarding job, and it's every day."

"Lifeguarding?" I asked. I couldn't believe it. *Lifeguarding?* "Well, you know, that's . . . good. That'll really help out with football."

"Is D.J. Schwenk being sarcastic?"

"No, I just . . . well, yeah, I was."

"Because you have to watch out. You keep making comments like that and sooner or later you'll have a sense of humor. And then you'll really be in trouble."

I smiled. I couldn't help myself. "Yeah, well. At least you'll be tan."

"Oh, don't you start too. Mom's already all over me about sunblock. She wants me dressed in a snowsuit or something."

I laughed. "Well, just thought I'd try. The training thing and all."

"Thanks for calling. Working with you was fun. Except for the parts that sucked."

"I thought it all sucked." I grinned.

"Nah, just parts. Thanks for calling."

After I hung up I sat on the bed still in my towel, thinking how nice that conversation had been. That's the thing about having someone to talk to. It's fun. I hate to compare Brian to Amber, but she and I didn't have conversations like that, at least not lately. Amber was pretty good at making fun of other people, but Brian—well, he did make fun of other people, like me not being able to talk or his mom and sunblock, but it wasn't mean. It was just fun. If I had to make a list of the very best qualities someone could have, that would be right at the top. Being nice-fun instead of mean-fun.

So I went to bed, and that nice feeling I'd had from talking to Brian, from talking, basically, slowly wore off as I realized I wouldn't have anyone to talk to. Or train. I couldn't go to Jimmy Ott and ask if he had any other football players in need of a workout. It'd taken everything I had just to call Brian. And there was certainly no one in Red Bend to go to and say I was a dumb girl farmer who'd flunked English and now wanted to be a sports trainer. Oh, they'd line up for that. The only person I could possibly come up with was Curtis, which wouldn't work for reasons you'll understand if you've ever had a brother.

Basically what it came down to was that my life sucked. It sucked even more than it had before Brian showed up, because now I knew it.

13

TALK

$\mathcal{M}$onday morning I decided that if I was going to spend my life as a cow, at least I'd be in good company. Besides, I like cows. Every time I changed the milking machine I'd rest my ear against the cow I was working on, listening to all that gurgling, and think to myself, This isn't so bad. And every time I'd convince myself a little bit more that it wasn't.

And then just as I was hooking up Tim Brown, named after a University of Notre Dame wide receiver, I heard a noise that didn't come from Tim's belly at all, and I looked up and almost jumped out of my skin, because there was Brian Nelson.

"Jeez!" I croaked. "What are you doing here?"

"Good to see you too."

Great beginning, D.J. "You just spooked me a little."

"I'm pretty spooky."

I couldn't think of one thing to say. Tim Brown flicked her tail in my ear just like a whip; I guess I'd given her a little tug without realizing it.

"I changed my mind," Brian said finally. "About training."

"Oh."

He kicked at the barn floor. "I started thinking you were right about lifeguarding."

"Oh," I said. Again.

"Aren't you going to say anything?"

"Um . . . I guess you should start with weights."

"That's not what I—" He sighed. "Okay." He picked up a curl bar.

I kept my head against Tim Brown, trying to figure out what just happened. I sure didn't want to make a big deal out of it—it was Brian's decision, after all, and I wasn't going to get gushy or anything. But boy oh boy, once it started to sink in . . .

"Brian? This'll be okay."

"Don't give yourself a heart attack or anything." But he smiled when he said it.

After milking, Brian walked the cows out with me, tossing Smut's football to her because she *was* giving herself a heart attack, she was so happy to see him. He sighed. "You know, there is one thing. It shouldn't bug me but it does . . ."

Uh-oh, I thought to myself, thinking of a million things he could name off.

"It's just—I know it's some passive-aggressive thing—but the silent treatment thing really bums me out."

"The passive what?" I had no idea what he was talking about. I guess when you're smart like Brian is and you get good grades you're allowed to go around using words that no one understands.

"You know. I say something and it's not what you want to hear so you wait and wait until I say the right thing."

I had to stop walking, I was so surprised. "What?"

"You do it all the time. Like just now when you said that I'd spooked you. I tried to make a joke, but you just waited and didn't say anything until I'd apologized."

"I—you think I did that on purpose?"

"Yeah. I mean, who else just sits there waiting like that?"

"You think I'm waiting?" This was getting old, me repeating everything he said. "It's because I don't know what to say! Or I'm trying to figure out what to say but by the time I get around to figuring it out you're talking again."

"Really?" Brian looked like he didn't believe me.

"Yeah! I mean, you talk like I'm smart or something, but really, you know, I'm . . . not."

That made him laugh.

"I'm serious."

"So when I say I hate weights and you don't say anything, you're really just trying to figure out how to tell me to shut up?" He grinned.

"That would be mean. I'm supposed to say encouraging things."

"Yeah, and I'm not supposed to be a jerk."

"You're not a jerk. Most of the time, anyway." I grinned.

"Huh. So how do I know when you're really mad at me?"

I thought so long that Brian rolled his eyes. "I guess," I said finally, "I'd make you clean the barn floor."

"I promise I won't make you mad," Brian said, so seriously that I cracked up.

I so, so, so wanted to show Brian my new football field, but because Dad was still around we had to paint instead. Which Brian didn't seem to mind too much, remarkably. He even went to work painting all that detail work around the windows. He was still super slow, but at least he didn't drip paint all over the glass the way I would have.

All of a sudden Dad came thumping into the barn with his cane, startling us both. "How do you two feel about walnuts?"

"Walnuts?" Brian asked.

"Yeah. In brownies." Like it was the most obvious thing in the world.

"It really doesn't matter," I said quickly, trying to get Dad out of there.

He ignored me. "What do you think, Rob?"

"Ah, sure, I love walnuts," Brian managed.

Dad sighed. "I'll have to pick some up." And he tapped his way out.

Brian looked so confused that I had to explain. "He got in a fight at church with some old lady and so now he's trying to prove that my mom makes better brownies."

"Does she?"

"No, she never makes them! So Dad's going to do it and say she did it because he doesn't want anyone to think a guy bakes."

Brian laughed. "They might be okay."

"Have you tasted my dad's cooking?"

"Maybe he'll add some of that Texas barbecue sauce, give them a little zip."

We both laughed at that.

When we went in for lunch, we were nearly knocked down by the thick warm smell of chocolate.

"Oh my God," Brian moaned.

Dad grinned like it was nothing. As soon as he brought the brownies to the table, though, you could tell there was a problem because he was serving them in bowls, which you don't normally encounter with that particular food. They oozed.

Brian dug into his so that brownie guts dripped down his chin. "These are great."

"What do you think?" Dad asked sharply, seeing my face.

"They're good. It's just . . . they're a little runny."

"Can I have another one?" Brian asked.

So Dad put the pan in the middle of the table and all three of us went to work with spoons until the pan was empty and we looked like a bunch of dirty-faced kids.

"You know what I think?" Brian frowned as he licked his fingers. "This really has to be a scientific process. You need to test a bunch of recipes, find the best one."

Dad nodded to himself. "You know, you're right."

"Oh, come on," I said. "You're kidding—"

Brian scowled at me, and, stupid as I am, I finally figured out what he was getting at. Recipes don't just need test bakers; they need test eaters too. And if I had to spend the next week eating brownies with a spoon, well, that was a sacrifice I was willing to make for my father.

"Don't forget the walnuts," Brian added helpfully.

"You really think so?" Dad thought about it.

"I've always felt walnuts are crucial to any baking project," Brian said, so seriously that I choked on my milk.

Curtis finally showed up, disappointed that we hadn't left him any brownies, but that's what you get for sleeping at someone else's house until whenever it was he slept. The second he and Dad left, I raced for the heifer field. "Come on! I have something to show you!"

Boy, you should have seen Brian's face. Bright green grass three inches high, lines sharp as rulers, corner flags fluttering away . . . pretty as a postcard. Except for the yearling pooping right there on the thirty-yard line.

"Norm, you moron!" I yelled. "Get off the field!"

Of course Brian cracked up, which I guess he had every right to do because I was laughing too, and then he gave the heifers a long lecture on where they could poop and where they couldn't. It was the funniest thing I'd ever seen, Brian standing there waving his finger like he was some kind of professor and all the heifers eyeing him, flicking the flies off their ears, like they were really paying attention. Until they pooped.

"You cut that out, Norm!" I shouted. "You do that some-where else!"

"What's that cow's name?" Brian asked.

"The heifer? Norm Van Brocklin."

"Who's that?"

"The first Vikings coach. Back in the sixties."

"How about that one?"

"Jerry Burns."

"I know him! He was a Viking coach too." Brian seemed pleased he knew that.

"That's what Dad wanted this year. Vikings staff."

"Why'd he use coaches instead of football players?"

I shrugged like I didn't know the answer. "I remember one year I showed a heifer named Lee Roy Jordan."

"You what?"

"You know, the 4-H fair? You must go sometimes for the carnival rides."

"You showed cows?" Brian looked amazed.

"Well, duh, look where we live. Lee Roy Jordan was some University of Alabama tackle from back in the sixties. These old farmers would pass by and see that name and light up. 'Remember the Orange Bowl? Remember that play?' I heard more about that one game . . ."

And that was how our days went. We painted and worked out and trained, and Rick Leach (Michigan) and Sidney Williams (Wisconsin) both calved, so we had little baby heifers to feed, which is more work but they're so cute it's worth it. Dad named them Max Winter and Bert Rose after the Vikings' first president and general manager from 1961 when Dad as a kid decided that a start-up team like that would need a player like him someday, which is how all us Schwenks ended up not being Packers fans. Brian brought a whole bunch of those little triangular flags from his dad's truck dealership and strung them around the field to keep the heifers off the grass, which made our football field look extra great. But mainly what I remember is talking. Eating brownies, lots of them, but mainly just talking. Being with Brian, it was like I was practicing something I'd never known I needed but I might need again sometime, so getting it down—figuring out how to talk—would probably be a good idea.

14

TALK BACK

I say that's how the week went, and it was pretty great in the beginning. But then things began to get a little intense. For one thing, Dad and the brownies—well, let's just say I never knew baking powder was so important. And then there was the subject of Curtis.

On Wednesday, Dad and Curtis had to go back to the dentist. Curtis had a cavity even though he flosses every night, which I find kind of unusual for a kid who's not all that big on personal hygiene. Dad was disgusted. "It's microscopic, for Pete's sake." He kept popping his teeth out to make the point. Which was something I really wanted Brian to see.

"It's important" was all Curtis would say.

Once they left we went out to work on Brian's arm. Again. As he passed me the football he asked, "How come Curtis never talks?"

"He talks," I said. "He talks to his friends, I think."

"You think?"

"He's not retarded," I said defensively.

"Of course he's not retarded! I didn't say he was retarded."

"They keep testing him at school. But he's not. There's nothing wrong with him."

Brian eyed me. "Why do you think they're testing him, then?"

"Move your feet more," I said for the millionth time. We passed the football for a few minutes, me not saying a word while I thought about all this.

"Never mind," Brian said finally. "Forget I said anything."

"So what do you think is wrong?" I asked.

"Nothing. I don't think it's anything. It's just, my mother . . ."

"Your mother thinks there's something wrong with Curtis?" I couldn't believe it.

"She's with this group called Talk Back. She goes all over Wisconsin talking to church groups."

"Talk Back? That's really what it's called? You're supposed to walk into some church basement and say, 'I'm here to learn how to Talk Back?'" It was a little mean, I know, but it made me mad, the thought of Brian and his mom sitting around talking about how screwed up Curtis was, and the rest of us too, probably.

"It's a stupid name, I know. It's just to get families communicating and stuff."

"Does it work?"

Brian shrugged. "I don't know. She's so busy helping families that she's never home. It's kind of funny, actually, that part of it." But he didn't look like he thought it was funny at all.

And then there was this long, awkward silence.

"Is that how you know about that passive thing you called me?" I had to ask.

"What, passive-aggressive? Yeah, I guess so."

That made me feel better, knowing there was a reason he knew fancy terms like that. He'd picked them up from his mother. "So is your mom like Oprah Winfrey?" I asked. Because that was the only person I could think of who would do stuff like trying to get families to talk to each other.

Brian nodded. "Yeah. In fact, my mom *is* Oprah Winfrey."

"She is not," I said. "Oprah Winfrey doesn't live in Wisconsin."

At that we both cracked up.

"So is your mom ever on her show?" I asked.

"Oh, all the time. They're like best friends."

Which made us laugh even more.

Once that whole Talk Back thing came out, though, I couldn't get it out of my mind. That image of Brian and his truck salesman dad and Oprah Winfrey sitting around the kitchen table, talking through family problems—sheesh. That was hard enough. But it also seemed like Oprah Winfrey was rubbing off on us too, and all our talk.

Friday morning as we were painting Brian said, "So, your brothers are working at a football camp, right?"

I shrugged.

"What's with you?" He waited but I didn't say anything. "Okay. Is this one of your 'I'm waiting for you to say something' silences or one of your 'I'm trying to figure out what to say' silences or one of your 'I don't want to talk about it' silences?"

"I don't want to talk about it."

"Okay. I just think you might want to talk about it. In our family we talk all the time."

"About my brothers?" I asked sarcastically.

"About problems. That's what you do in a family—you talk about things."

"And all that talk makes you happy?"

There was a bit of a silence. "Drop dead," he said.

And we didn't say anything else until lunchtime, when things kind of went back to normal.

Jogging that afternoon, Brian asked what I was up to for the weekend and I said, "Nothing," which pretty much summed it up, and then just to be polite I asked what he was doing.

He sighed. "Colleges. We already went out a couple of times, but I'm narrowing it down now, and I want to talk to coaches before the season starts . . ."

Silence.

"Why aren't you saying anything?"

"What? It's great, your looking at colleges. That's real important."

"Why? Aren't you thinking about that stuff?"

I had to laugh, but it wasn't one of those laughs like it was funny. It was one of the laughs like it wasn't. "A, we can't afford it. B, I'm only going to be a junior, and C . . ." I didn't want to bring up C.

"What do you mean, you can't afford it? Your brothers are going."

"Yeah, on football scholarships. Which if you haven't noticed I can't get."

"There's basketball. You should be able to get something, at least."

"Yeah, well, they don't like it too much when you miss your sophomore year because your dad won't get a stupid operation. And they also don't like too much those big fat F's on your transcript." It's funny, part of me didn't want Brian to know in a million years about my failing, but the other part felt it was really important to tell him.

"They'd understand about your dad—wait, an F? You flunked a class?" Brian was so surprised he stopped running. I kept walking, at least, because I had to do something.

"Yup. Sophomore English." I kicked a stone out of the road.

"But you're not—come on—"

"You mean I'm not a total idiot?"

"That's not what I meant." Though it kind of was.

"Me and Curtis, a couple of morons. Wouldn't your mother have fun with us."

"Come on, stop it. What happened?"

I kicked another stone. "Nothing. I was supposed to write these papers and I didn't because I was so busy with the farm, and I flunked."

"If you wrote the papers could they change it? The grade?"

"They say they can, but I'm not writing them, so it really doesn't matter, does it?"

"I'll write them if you want," he offered like it was the most casual thing in the world.

I stopped and stared at him.

"What?"

"You don't even know what they're about."

"It doesn't matter. You just sling it the right way. The words, I mean," he added.

"I know . . ." It just knocked me out, that Brian could just write a paper like that, just "sling it" when the only thing I knew how to sling was cow poop. Maybe I was a moron.

"Hey," Brian offered, "at least you don't have Jimmy Ott telling everyone what a bum you are."

And that cheered me up—it really did. It reminded me of how Jimmy sent Brian over in the first place, and how much Jimmy liked me and all of us Schwenks even though we don't talk much and can't write about Shakespeare.

At that moment what I really wanted was for Brian to put his arm around my shoulders the way they do in TV ads. But that pretty clearly wasn't going to happen, so instead I punched him, right there at the bottom of his deltoid where it felt nice and solid, and then Smut came tearing down the road to see us and Brian left for the day. For his big senior year college trip, while I stayed on the farm doing nothing.

I kind of figured that once he left my brain would go back to the I-am-a-cow business, and sure enough it did. It started right away at dinner, when I noticed how tired Mom looked. Now that I thought about it, she was a cow too. Just as much as me or the checkout ladies at the supermarket. She didn't want that extra job, but when they asked her to do it she took it without even thinking she could say no. She walked right into that milking stall of a principal's office.

That made me really depressed, as depressed as the thought of me as a cow, I guess because it didn't give me much to look forward to. It's one thing thinking that you're a cow when you're a teenager or a farmer, or a checkout lady. But Mom had a real job, with a real office — at least until they hired the permanent principal — and a real classroom she taught in, and her life sounded even worse than mine. She'd had all that time to find something to do with her life, and this is what she ended up with?

So you can see how cheery I was.

Then in bed I started thinking about Win and Bill and *their* lives, what I knew about them, anyway. It sounds stupid at first, but when you think about it, football players don't have it much better. They do what you tell them to do, they stand where you tell them to stand, and the whole point of it is to produce something for other people. No one plays football just because they love the game. I mean, they do love it, but anyone could do that, even guys who stink. Football players play so people can watch them and get excited and buy tickets and clothing and stuff. So people will have something to talk about on Monday mornings. And it's not like football players get treated any better than cows do. Sure, they get doctors just like cows get vets. But when they're old and hurt like my dad is, there's not some big old wallet of money from people saying, Thank you for feeding us all that excitement and tickets and stuff to watch on TV. Last year Bill was friends with a tackle who tore up his knee, and they kicked him right out of college. He couldn't feed them anything anymore. If that's not the same as leading a cow into a cattle dealer's truck, I don't know what is.

Then I started thinking that maybe everyone in the whole world was just like a cow, and we all go along doing what we're supposed to without complaining or even really noticing, until we die. Stocking groceries and selling cars and teaching school and cashing checks and raising kids, all these jobs that people just one day start doing without even really thinking about it, walking right into their milking stall the way that heifers do after they've had their first calf and start getting milked for the first time. Until we die. And maybe that's all there is to life.

And that's what I thought about all night long. All this stuff you never hear on *Oprah Winfrey*, which you can understand because if I got on the show and started talking, everyone in the audience would probably kill themselves.

15

EPIPHANY

As you might imagine, the weekend went downhill from there.

The next morning when I came in from milking, Mom and Dad were rushing around like the house was on fire as Curtis sat there in his baseball uniform eating breakfast. I guess I should have mentioned before now that his big state Little League quarterfinals were today. And that this was a big deal, and someone had sent over a bunch of good luck balloons, and that my folks were planning to drive to Green Bay in a caravan with other families and fans. The whole thing. But you know what? This isn't Curtis's story, it's mine. And by this point I was pretty sick of Little League. Because if it weren't for baseball he and I would be managing the farm just fine, and then Jimmy Ott never would have sent Brian over to help us out and so I wouldn't know that my life and everyone's life was just like a cow's, and I wouldn't have to think about Brian's Oprah Winfrey mother and whatever it is she says about Curtis never talking, and all in all my life would be a whole lot simpler.

"Aren't you going to wish Curtis good luck?" Mom asked. Dad gave me a look.

So I said, "Hope you win," just wanting them gone so much.

But when they left I felt like I was on a deserted island or something, I was so alone. I couldn't even nap. I kept thinking about Brian on his fancy college tour, and eventually just to torture myself I went over to my desk and read through the letters I'd gotten.

It's not a desk, really, it's my Grandma Joyce's sewing table, but we took out the sewing machine to make room for my legs. I'd kept all my letters from college basketball coaches. Most were just computer-printout letters they'd sent a thousand girls. But I got a few just to me from coaches who'd come to my games, asking me to keep them posted about how I was doing and my upcoming year and everything. And then one letter, the worst one, was from a coach who I guess had called the school later, and she wrote saying that she was sorry but because I'd quit she couldn't look at me anymore because there were so many other good players out there who could at least finish a season. That was her point, anyway.

So there were my prospects for college, all shot to pieces.

And then because I wasn't feeling bad enough already, I dug out all the stuff from Mrs. Stolze's English class, the list of papers I never wrote and her letters about how much trouble I was in. At the back of the file were some letters she'd sent Mom even, saying maybe we should go to family counseling.

I sat there for a long time trying to figure out how counseling would have helped. I didn't need to talk; I needed to write those papers. The more I thought about it, the more I thought that someone like Brian's Oprah Winfrey mom wouldn't be able to help our family one bit except make us feel bad, and seeing how bad I already felt, I didn't think I needed to feel any worse.

Eventually I went to bed and Smut lay next to me even though she's not supposed to be upstairs, but I sure was glad to have her, her head on my belly, looking at me with sad eyes while I just felt worse and worse, so bad that I wanted to talk to Brian even though I didn't want him to know any of this stuff, and anyway I was thinking about him too much, and if nothing else it just reminded me that he was looking at colleges and I never would.

I guess I fell asleep, because the next thing I knew it was time for milking, and then after milking because I couldn't think of anything else to do I drove the pickup into town. There was a huge banner up saying "Good Luck Red Bend Expos"—that's Curtis's team—and signs in some of the store windows and all sorts of garbage. I didn't know what to do, so I went over to Jorgensen's Ice Cream Stand where Kari worked and hung out with her for a while. We talked about the upcoming volleyball season, which you can tell I care about a whole lot because whenever I bring it up I say how much it sucks. We don't have that great a team and I don't like our coach at all. Plus we kept getting interrupted, families coming in just like cows for their little family treats, getting just the flavors you'd expect them to get because no one ever thinks about doing something different for just one night.

So I was in a great mood.

Then Amber came in, and she *was* in a great mood. You think I'd be thrilled to see her seeing as she's my best friend, but I wasn't, I guess because I'd been thinking how we weren't really that close. We talked but we never *talked* like Talk Back talk. I'd wanted to tell her so much about all my thoughts about people being stuck in their roles just like cows, but the minute I opened my mouth she just squashed me down.

So anyway, she right away started telling Kari and me about the wedding she'd just worked, some born-agains who didn't drink or smoke or dance or anything so everyone went home right after the cake was served after gobbling down every bit of food because they were all so bored. Normally I'd love this story and Amber would tell it a couple times just to get it right. But that night I didn't care. I mean, in the whole scope of existence, does it really matter if you have beer at your wedding? Will it change when you die, or how important your life will be when you look back on it?

Right about then someone came in with the news that the Red Bend Expos had lost their game, which you'd think I'd want to hear but I didn't. So I went home and lay in the dark until I heard Mom and Dad and Curtis come back. Mom looked in at me but I pretended to be asleep so I wouldn't have to talk to anyone.

The next day, Sunday, was even worse.

When I came in from milking, Mom was getting all ready for church, hustling around Curtis, and Dad was arranging brownies on a plate and telling Mom what the ingredients were in case anyone asked. They really wanted me to go with them, but that wasn't going to happen. I just went back upstairs to bed. When I came down later after a nap that didn't help one little bit, they'd come back from church and Dad was taking a big casserole out of the oven.

"What's that?" I asked.

"Chicken."

"What are those black things?"

"Prunes." He shot me a warning look not to say anything.

So I didn't. But there was no way on this earth I was going to eat *prunes* and *chicken* mixed together. And that set the stage for Sunday dinner.

During dinner Mom kept talking about all the people at church who'd congratulated Curtis, which kind of doesn't make sense because Red Bend lost. But it was a big deal, Red

Bend making it to the quarterfinals, and I guess Curtis played well. Plus Dad had brought his brownies to the game and everyone loved them, plus they loved them at church too, even though by this time I'd had enough brownies to last me a couple years. But Mom was saying how she could write out the recipe in her handwriting and copy it for everyone who wanted it, making it sound like no one in the entire town of Red Bend could survive for even one more day if they didn't have Mom's brownies that were really made by Dad.

Then there was this little silence and Mom looked at me. "D.J.?"

"Yeah?" I said, eating all the rolls because I wasn't going to touch those prunes.

"There's an awards ceremony in two weeks in Madison. For Little League. And, well, I've got a board meeting and you know Dad can't drive. So we were hoping you could take Curtis."

Curtis, hearing this, tried basically to crawl under the table.

"I don't know," I answered. But I was thinking I'd rather die than sit with one-word-a-month Curtis in our crappy old Caravan for ten hours driving there and back, just to be stuck in Madison around a bunch of smart rich kids from the University of Wisconsin, which I couldn't get into in a million years, to listen to an assistant coach for some minor league team in Iowa tell a roomful of really bored kids how important teamwork is while their parents all sat there wishing they served beer at these things.

"I don't know," I said. "Who's going to milk?"

"I can handle it," Dad said. "Me and Brendan could do it."

"Brendan?" I put my fork down. "His name's *Brian*. Brian Nelson. Is that so hard? Listen: B. R. I. A. N. Can you manage that?"

"Darlene Joyce," Mom said in a warning voice.

"Why don't you get mad at *him*? Why don't once in your life you get mad at him!" I stood up.

"You sit yourself right back down, young lady," Dad said.

"You can all—" I was going to say "go to hell," but, you know, even when you're angry, there's this line you don't cross. Not on Schwenk Farm. So I just stomped out instead.

I spent the afternoon out in the north hay field. Smut came with me. She's so great. If I had to choose between driving somewhere with Curtis or with Smut, she'd be so much my first choice. So what if she can't talk, at least she can show that she likes you and that she's listening to you, and that she's happy or sad. It occurred to me, sitting there, that I had a little brother who wasn't even equipped to be a dog.

It wasn't that I minded so much about going to the awards thing. I'd been to about a million awards ceremonies for Win and Bill, and for me too. It was going to Madison and having it rubbed in my face that I was poor and stupid and ugly and just not cool at all. It's one thing knowing that in Red Bend.

But it's another thing in a real city with a bunch of people who aren't, and who never were, and who never will be any of those things, and who probably never thought about how they were cows, and who if you analyzed their lives probably weren't.

After a while I got hungry, but there was no way I was going back inside. So I went down to the road, the long way that doesn't go past the house, and found a half-dozen tomatoes someone had left in the mailbox. The first couple were okay, but then it turned into a whole bunch of tomatoes that I had to force down without salt or anything.

Then I went in the barn from the other side so no one would see me and set up for milking, and let the cows in and got the milking done, hoping like anything that no one would come out, and the good news is that because my family doesn't ever talk about anything, no one did, and I wasn't forced into an Oprah Winfrey moment or anything awful like that. Then I let the cows out and cleaned the barn and waited in the hayloft, totally bored by now, for all the lights to go off so I could go back inside.

And when I did I was so hungry, I ate all the leftover chicken. Even the prunes. And if there'd been another whole pan I would have eaten that too.

You'd think that I'd be really happy to see Brian on Monday morning, seeing as I tended to be happy when he was around and unhappy when he wasn't. But I sure didn't want to talk about his college trip or his therapist mother or anything at all, really. So we didn't say anything when he showed up and he just started on his weights. Then Dad and Curtis headed out to PT so we could start our workout right away, which was good because if I'd had to paint for a couple hours I don't think I would have survived.

I hadn't done anything all weekend unless you count sulking, but I guess my body needed the rest. So after we jogged up to the heifer field, we started this thing where I'd stand behind Brian and run out to his passes. You'd be surprised how well this worked. Plus Brian's aim seemed to be getting better, or maybe I was just moving to the ball more. He'd call out how far I had to run and I'd race off.

We started with five- or ten-yard passes and really got into a rhythm. It reminded me of when I played receiver against Bill. He'd let me catch about half of Win's passes so I didn't get demoralized. Then he'd tackle me. But I got pretty good at catching a football. Besides, it's not that hard. I'd watch how Win, or Curtis later, released it, and it's pretty obvious where the ball is going to end up. It's not going to swerve midflight or anything like that. All you have to do is make it to where the ball's headed at the same time the ball does, preferably without your huge older brother getting there first.

So I'd catch the ball and jog it back to Brian, and we'd do it again. And it was the strangest thing, but every time Brian

passed me the ball I felt a little better. Like one of those films
of the little seed growing out of the ground and its leaves un-
curl and then it grows a flower. Which isn't a very good de-
scription because if you think about it long enough in terms
of football you kind of picture the flower getting smushed.
But that's how I felt. Maybe it was remembering how much
fun I used to have with Bill and Win. Or that I was getting off
my butt, finally. Brian was in a good mood too, I think because I was catching his passes.

"Okay," he said with a grin, setting me up for a big play.
"Ready? Thirty-five yards. Line up . . . Hut one — hut two —
hut three — Go!" And I took off sprinting, glancing over my
shoulder just enough to see where the football was headed
way down the field, and I started to run. And as I ran I had
this wonderful memory of the 4 x 100 back when I was a
freshman, when I was anchor leg and standing there on the
track all nervous waiting for the gun to go off, and then when
it did watching the first leg start, and the first baton handoff,
and the second, all the time wanting so bad to run myself
and feeling so nervous but less nervous the closer and closer
the baton got, until I could see Amy Hagendorf coming
around the far turn pumping away with all her might, her
hair going everywhere and her face screwed up like she was
trying to remember something really important, and she'd
get closer and closer to me, that baton in her hand, and I'd
turn with my hand out behind me, waiting for her, and with

all her breath she'd gasp out, "Go!" and I'd start to run—not too fast even though my legs wanted to take me out of there—until I felt that cold baton hit my hand, and my fingers would curl around it and just then, just at that moment, I'd stop worrying and just start flying, my legs pumping away without me even thinking, straight for the finish line.

That's what I was remembering as I ran down the heifer field, and thinking how this was even better because my legs didn't have to wait, they could stretch out as much as they wanted with that feeling like I could run forever. And I looked up, right at the perfect moment, and there was the football coming down. And I put out my hands and caught it like the raw egg at an egg toss, caught it like a little baby, and tucked it under my arm, and then because I was feeling so good I just kept running as fast as I ever could right to the goal line. I sprinted right over it and banked into a turn and jogged back, feeling . . . perfect. Like life, no matter how much it sucked, every once in a while came together and was just perfect.

With a big grin and still panting a little, I handed the football to Brian, who was grinning right back at me. He slapped me on the back. "God damn! I sure am glad I'm not playing against you."

And he said a whole bunch of other stuff but I didn't hear a single word because a huge idea was exploding inside me, taking up so much space that there wasn't any room left for air or blood or listening or anything else. I went back next to Brian and waited for his call and his pass, but I couldn't tell you one thing that happened because I was so busy thinking I didn't notice.

And that's—if you're wondering, that's when it happened. That's when I decided I was going to play on the Red Bend, Wisconsin, High School Football Team.

16

HEIFERS DON'T PLAY
FOOTBALL

I bet right now you're saying, "She's doing *what?*" Which I guess I'd be saying if I was in your shoes. A girl wanting to play football? Maybe I really was crazy.

But you have to remember, I wasn't all that bad a football player. I mean, it was a realistic thing—more realistic for me than ballet, say. (Just the thought of me doing ballet makes me laugh.) I grew up in a football family, I played football with my brothers who are all really, really good football players, and I played Pee Wee football pretty much up into junior high, when it got a little weird and I started volleyball instead. Plus I've been to every Red Bend football game in my entire life, so I knew all the players and most of the players on the other teams too. Not that I had their playbooks, but you understand.

So it wasn't like I didn't know anything about football or how to play it. And I was strong and big. Not as big as Win or Bill, or Curtis lately, but I could hold my own. It's not like this is the pros. This is a pretty small town with a pretty small school. Every once in a while you see a movie about high school football where the actors are all enormous — they're all big enough to play in the NFL. Hasn't anyone in Hollywood ever been to a real high school? Half the guys there are fourteen or fifteen years old; they're not going to be all that big when they're grown up because they're like normal, and they're not even done growing. I'm bigger than almost all the guys in school, which up until now wasn't something I was too pleased about. If I was a guy I'd make a pretty decent lineman, here in Red Bend. Plus I'm fast. I wouldn't be the fastest but I was fast enough to make Brian sweat, and I knew I could make some other guys sweat too.

I wouldn't be the first girl in the world to play football either. You hear stories sometimes about high school girls who place kick, which is safe and neat and you don't get tackled or anything. And I saw a TV thing once about a football league made of girls in California or someplace like that. But I'd never heard of a girl playing running back on a boys' team. Which was the position I wanted to play.

But the real reason I wanted to play football — and I sure wanted it as much as I've ever wanted anything in my life, as much as I wanted to beat Hawley in basketball last season — is because, well, this is going to sound really strange, and I'll probably never be able to explain to anyone. But if I made the Red Bend football team, it would mean I wasn't a cow. That's what I'd been struggling with ever since Brian showed up. Everyone I looked at, their whole lives, did exactly what they were supposed to do without even questioning it, without even wondering if they could do something different. Of course my brothers played football; everyone knew they'd be playing football. People knew before they were born, even. They never had a choice. They acted like cows do, doing what they're told without even thinking about it. But what if it was different? I mean, what if one day a cow out there in our pasture said to herself, "I've been looking at that tree for years and today I'm going to climb it"? Which wouldn't be all that safe for a cow to do, and which now that I think about it doesn't reflect too well on my own goals for football. But at least she'd be doing something, her very own idea.

And so would I. I'd be doing something. Even though we didn't have any money and I'm a failure at school—because that's what F means, it means failure—and I'll probably never go to college and I'm not pretty or popular or talkative or anything like that, I'd still be doing something. Something no other girl had ever done, no girl that I ever knew, anyway.

It's not like I stood there in our heifer field thinking all this through. Someone else's brain might work that fast, but mine sure doesn't. But I just had this immediate feeling that filled me up like milk pouring into a pitcher until you can see it right there at the rim almost bubbling out. That's what it felt like. It took me a lot longer to put the words to it. Some of the words I didn't figure out until just now, writing this down.

But I must have been thinking something, because Brian asked if I was okay.

"I'm fine."

"You look like you just remembered something," he said.

"It's nothing," I said. "Come on. Let's see some real distance now." And we went right back into the passing drills because I sure wasn't going to tell him. Not yet, anyway.

For the rest of the day my mind was going a million miles a minute: how I'd find gear to train in, how I'd train because it was only two weeks now until preseason, whether I'd make the team, what it would feel like to play in a real game . . . like I was in a room full of presents and I didn't know which one to open first.

On our run, Brian asked finally, "What's going on?"

"What do you mean?" I asked, kind of startled to be interrupted.

"You haven't said a word all day! Usually you say something, at least."

"Sorry."

"Are you mad about something?"

"No."

He looked at me.

"I'm not mad!" I figured I should say something more, and I'd been meaning to ask this for a while anyway. "What does your mom think is wrong with Curtis?"

"Oh. She doesn't think there's anything wrong with him. She just thinks it's real interesting that he never talks."

"What do you mean, 'interesting'?" I asked.

"I don't know. She just said that a lot of times in families people don't talk because they're afraid to."

I didn't say anything. I had this feeling that the more I thought about it, the more I'd see that Mrs. Oprah Winfrey Nelson was right.

But even that couldn't take away that bubbly feeling I had about football. It's like—the only way I can describe it is, well, you know that little guy in the tire ads, the one made out of big white cushions? That's what I felt like. Like I had big soft pillows all around me to protect me from a whole bunch of stuff that I hadn't been able to deal with before. It was like this totally crazy idea, *my* idea, was a shield keeping me safe from a whole bunch of pain.

I know that doesn't make any sense. Maybe it was just that I was so preoccupied with my own new set of problems, meaning football, that I didn't have too much time to think about anyone else's. But the thing is, I did think about them. All through milking when I wasn't thinking about all the stuff I needed to do, I thought about Curtis. He never talked around Dad, which I could understand completely. But Curtis didn't talk to me either. I didn't like that thought too much. Now that I thought about it, there was a lot of stuff about Curtis I didn't know.

Like why he's so into skulls. Which I haven't mentioned before because I never think about it except when I'm in his room, which I'm never in because of the skulls and because, well, how much time would you spend hanging out with your little brother who's suddenly taller than you and doesn't shower too much and never talks?

But I had to go into his room—he was on *another* sleepover. Probably trying to get away from Dad and a grumpy big sister (which I have to admit I was a lot). So he was gone and I needed to find some football gear to wear because I hadn't had any in about five years and I wanted to find out, you know, if it fit me because you can't play football without gear. So I had to go into his room, and then I saw the skulls again.

Curtis collects animal skulls. If there's a dead raccoon or something he'll take the head—hopefully it's so dead there's not much stuff stuck to it, yuck—and clean it all out and keep the skull. Mom caught him boiling something a couple years ago and she just let him keep that pot, bought herself another one. He's got that pot in his room now, along with about twenty skulls. And it's got to be both parts, you know—the head plus the jaw. Win brought him the head part of a deer once and Curtis wouldn't take it because it didn't have a jaw. But he's found another deer head since then. Skull, I mean. It's about the weirdest thing I've ever heard of. His little room is pretty ripe, what with the skulls— even though most of them are really old and dried out—and his clothes and all. I was glad to get out of there, after I'd found an old helmet and some cleats and a jersey in his closet under a whole bunch of junk.

Then I went into Win and Bill's room, which was just as weird. Compared to Curtis's room, it was neat as a pin. Two twin beds with matching covers, football posters on the walls, a corkboard with pictures of some of Bill's old girlfriends, Win's All-State plaque . . . It was like a model of a bedroom. If you wanted to do a magazine article about a room for two college football players, that's what it would look like. It wasn't a room for people. It was a room for people who were never coming home. That's what it felt like. I snuck around in there as quiet as a mouse because I didn't want Mom coming up and asking what I was doing with an armful of football gear and no explanation in the world. Luckily she didn't.

So I got to my room and locked the door and tried everything on. Here are a couple things I learned: Whatever kind of breasts you have, at least if they're, you know, kind of normal or less than normal like mine are, well, it doesn't matter because they don't show under the pads. Also, ponytails don't work too well with a helmet. Maybe some pro player somewhere has a ponytail and a custom-made helmet, but Curtis's Red Bend Junior High School helmet made my ponytail dig right into my spine in a way that would not work ever. I even tried letting my hair out, which I normally don't do because my neck gets so sweaty, and immediately my neck started getting sweaty. So I'd have to figure that out. Otherwise everything fit pretty well, all things considered. It's a lot of bulk. It's not like anyone ever says, I'm going to the movies and I'm going to wear my shoulder pads and thigh pads and hip pads and knee pads and rib pads and collar and helmet because they're so darn comfortable. On the plus side, when you're playing at least you know it slows everyone else down too. That's the only consolation. That and the fact that without it you'd probably get killed.

That night in bed I started getting second thoughts about how the kids at school would react. Or Amber. I hoped she'd think it was a good idea, but I can never tell what she'll say. Or Dad—jeez. The thought made my stomach hurt. Of course, Dad would find out eventually, if I made the team and all. He goes to every game and he'd notice after a while that there was a player on the bench named Schwenk, and he'd figure out it was me. But I didn't want to think about that part, him watching me play. That was too much. I just knew he couldn't find out in the next two weeks. It would be ten times worse than him finding out about me training Brian. I couldn't even think about the cracks he'd make. He didn't want anyone knowing he baked brownies—what would he say about a girl playing football?

And then there was my hair. I was thinking I might have to cut it because of the helmet and all. Amber was the obvious person, but I didn't want to tell her why, or lie, which she'd see right through. Plus I had a feeling she wouldn't do the best job in the world. No one would, not in Red Bend, anyway. I mean, have you ever heard anyone say they're heading over to Red Bend, Wisconsin, because people there cut hair so good? No, you haven't. And I felt if I was going to play boys' football I needed hair that didn't look like it'd been cut with a hedge trimmer.

But you know, even worrying about haircuts couldn't depress me. Because every time I started sinking low, I'd just remember about football. All this time I'd thought I wanted to be a trainer, when it turned out I wanted to be a player instead. I saw something I wanted to do and I decided to do it. The feeling of freedom this gave me—I can't even describe it. It was my decision. I chose it. I am not a cow.

17

Family Secrets

That cushiony feeling stayed with me too, keeping me safe so I wouldn't get smashed down by whatever came my way. It was the strangest thing. And because I had it, I could talk. Brian and I were already, you know, talking up a storm about a bunch of heavy stuff. But now we really let it rip.

And painting, well, if you ever want to talk to someone, painting a barn is a good way to do it. Tuesday, for example, we were stuck in there all morning. We started out chatting about how fast the calves were growing and whether Dad would keep making brownies, with lots of quiet time in between, good quiet. Then Brian asked kind of sadly, right out of the blue, "Do your folks get along?"

I thought about it a bit. "Yeah, they do. But they shouldn't."

He cracked up. He was laughing so hard he had to put down his roller.

Normally—like every single day of my life up to this point—I would have left it at that, because who wants to take someone feeling bad and make them feel worse? But for one thing I felt like we'd been spending a lot of time talking about my family, which is certainly worth talking about if you're looking for subjects, so I felt it was only fair to talk about his for a while. And frankly, I cared too.

So after we'd enjoyed Brian's good mood for a bit I asked, "Why? Do yours?"

He shrugged. "I think they're just waiting for me to go to college so they can split up."

"Jeez." I felt sick all of a sudden, like when Amber brings up her dad.

"It's not that big a deal," he said, sounding almost like he meant it.

"Does it," I asked, taking a big deep breath, "have anything to do with, you know, Talk Back and all of that?"

Brian painted for a bit. "They don't have anything to say to each other. All Mom ever wants to do is talk about feelings, what everyone's feeling. How we all have to get in touch with our feelings."

"You're pretty good at that," I said. "At least with football."

"What does that mean?"

Darn, I wished I hadn't opened my big fat mouth. "Nothing. It's just, you know, when you play you're always, you know, expressing your feelings." That's just great. A guy starts telling you his family secrets and you point out how he acts like a jerk. Good job, D.J.

"What does your dad do after games?" he asked.

"After football games?"

"Yeah. Whatever."

I thought about it. "He's like a coach: 'You messed that up, next time you need to . . .' That sort of thing."

Brian scowled. "My dad tells me how good I was, that I was perfect."

"And that's bad?" It sounded pretty fantastic to me.

"He really wanted me to take that lifeguarding job. He was real mad when I told him I was coming back here."

"I'm sorry. I wish we could pay you—"

"No! Remember that first week when I quit during haying? When I got home, he told me how smart I was, how I had to save my hands. But . . . you didn't quit."

"We couldn't."

"I know you couldn't! It's life and death for you guys." He frowned at himself.

"I wasn't being so great to you back then." Which I offered as a big gift to him, and it was quite a confession for me to make, if you want to know the truth.

But he didn't even take it. "My dad—he always says what I'm doing is right whether it is or not. But your dad expects it to be right."

I struggled through what Brian just said. "But Dad never says anything nice to us."

"So what? He knows you can do it. My father would never send three kids out haying. He'd hire someone. Or painting this barn. This is a big responsibility."

Yeah, I thought to myself. Too big.

"Your dad thinks a lot more of you than my dad does of me," Brian said softly.

Wow. On the one hand it was kind of nice, having someone tell me Dad's okay. That's not something I hear very much, and it was nice considering he's my father and he made me and all. Half of me, anyway.

But the more I thought about it, the angrier I got. Anyone could look at Dad and think he was just a funny guy who named his cows after football players and made brownies. But that wasn't the full picture. Besides, it wasn't that he believed I was good at anything. He just didn't have much of a choice.

"Actually," I said, "he's a real jerk."

"Oh, come on—"

"You want to know why I don't talk to Win and Bill?" I asked, and saying it—you know on nature shows sometimes they have the wild animal, the lion, in the cage, and they open the cage door real fast and the lion comes out? That's what it felt like. "Because they had a huge fight over Christmas and Bill and Win left and we haven't spoken to them since."

"Jeez," said Brian. "What was the fight about?"

That, strangely enough, is a tough question. Because in our family the fights are about weird things, weird little things. Like the time Bill forgot to clear his plate and Mom got screaming hysterical to the point her face turned purple and she wouldn't come out of her room for the rest of the night, even when Dad tried talking to her. Although we've all been really good about clearing our plates since then.

"It was stupid. Win was saying he didn't think he'd get drafted, and Dad made a crack about how he wasn't working hard enough. And Win said that if Dad worked half as hard at farming as Win did at football, maybe the farm would break even. And then Dad got real mad and said it was going to be their farm someday, and Win said he didn't want it."

I worked with my roller for a bit, remembering what came next, Dad's exact words: If you're so damn unhappy, why don't you clear out now? And Win stood up and glared at Dad and went right upstairs. And then Bill went up too, leaving Curtis and me staring at our plates, and finally Mom went up to talk to them I guess, and I cleared the table, and Win and Bill came down with their bags.

"So they both left," I continued. "And it's all Dad's fault."

"So why aren't you talking to them?" Brian asked finally.

I slapped some paint on my roller, which was tough because my eyes were watery all of sudden. "Because before they left, Bill asked me which side I was on."

Brian didn't say a word. Just waited. That impressed me so much.

"It wasn't fair, him asking that. I have to live here for two more years at least. I can't get Dad all mad at me. It wasn't fair," I whispered. "It wasn't fair."

"But it's been like seven months. Couldn't you call?"

I painted for a while. "Because I'm not the one who has to apologize." That's a bruise Bill will have to punch first, I thought to myself.

We didn't say anything for a long, long time. Just painted.

"Can I ask a question?" Brian asked finally. "Did your dad play college ball?"

I snorted. "Until he flunked out. But he played a lot in the army."

Brian gave me this weird look.

"What?" I asked.

"It's just interesting, the parallels. What happened with you at school last year."

For a moment I almost threw my brush at him, I was so mad. But I just kept painting. "Is that what your mom would say?" I asked, trying to sound mature.

"I think so. I didn't mean to make you mad," he offered after a couple minutes. I guess it was pretty obvious.

"I'd just never thought about it before," I said.

"You can get mad at me if you want."

"If I did, you'd be covered in paint."

Which made us both laugh, and broke that horrible tension a little, gave me time to get my padding back. And I did, a bit. Enough to remember that at least I didn't flunk out of *college*, I just failed one stupid class.

After a while, just to fill up all that silence, I said, "I'm sorry you don't get along with your dad."

"That's the thing, I do get along with him. But now I—I kind of wish I didn't."

"You could have my dad instead," I offered. Which made us both grin.

"Do I really sound that bad when I'm playing?" It sounded like it took as much courage for him to ask that as some of my questions.

"What's your dad say?" I asked. Which I thought was very smart and Oprah-like.

"He always says it's their fault, the other players. Whenever we talk about it."

I nodded. That explained a lot.

"What"—Brian kind of steeled himself—"what would your dad say?"

I knew what my dad would say because I'd heard him say it, heard him rant about what a useless whiner Brian was, tell Jimmy Ott to kick him off the team. He'd said worse than that too, especially that night Brian had made so much fun of Bill. After that game Bill went out back with a sledgehammer and just demolished an old broken tiller we had. Reduced it to bits. Dad sure had some things to say about Brian then.

"He'd say"—I chose my words extra carefully—"that a team starts with its QB."

Brian shook his head. "You have no idea how much Jimmy Ott talks about your brothers. Especially Win. It makes my dad so mad. He says it's unprofessional. And it made me want to just kill Red Bend. Even though Jimmy, he isn't doing it to be mean or get us riled up. He's just making a point."

"Oh," I said.

"About attitude. Your brothers' attitude. I think it made me so mad because I knew he was really making the point to me."

We thought that over for a while. Then, because I couldn't stand it any longer, I had to ask, "Do you think I was just copying my dad when I, you know, screwed up in English?"

Brian sighed. "That's what my mom would say. She sees that stuff everywhere. Like, 'Oh, you're driving a *red* car?' So what? It was probably just real hard for you, with school and the farm and all."

"My teacher said our family should, you know, talk to someone." I focused on my painting so I wouldn't have to look at him when I said it.

"Like a counselor?" Brian asked, surprised.

"I guess so. I didn't even know she'd said it until a couple days ago."

"Wow." Brian chuckled a little.

"What?"

"It's just funny. Here you are being told that you need a family counselor when I've got that already. Too bad Jimmy Ott couldn't send me to some jock to straighten out my football." Suddenly he stopped laughing. "But I guess that's what he did, isn't it?"

And that was so strange to even think about that we barely said another word until Dad and Curtis left and we went up to the heifer field and ran our guts out. And the good thing about our conversation—well, one of the good things, one of the good obvious things—is that it gave me an excuse. Because halfway through when we were both panting and sweaty, my clothes soaking wet and Brian's hair stuck to his forehead, he asked why I was doing the workout too.

"Because I'm your goddam therapist," I gasped.

18

D.J. Goes to Town

Wednesday morning I decided that if I was really going to spend the next two weeks training for preseason, I should probably figure out if I would even, you know, be allowed to play. So after Brian worked through his weights and stretches, I said we could quit for the day. He gave me this long look but I wouldn't look back because I'm such a bad liar, so eventually he left and I took the pickup to Home Depot to track down Jeff Peterson.

Jeff Peterson works in the flooring department there, but his other job, his real job if you ask anyone including him, is coaching Red Bend football. He's been doing it for three years and he was assistant coach for a long while before that. He and Bill were really close when Bill was in high school, and he really helped Bill with all the scholarship stuff and getting his grades in order. He has a little mustache, and whenever he's thinking hard he'll chew on it, sort of pull his upper lip down and gnaw on it a little. I bet he doesn't even notice when he does it. Bill and Win used to have a great time imitating him. He's a good guy. He doesn't yell. I like that.

Sure enough, there he was in the flooring department, growing out his mustache for football season. He was helping some lady decide between four identical colors of carpet until finally she went away without buying anything and he turned to me.

"Hey there, Coach," I said.

"Well, hey there, D.J. What can I do you for?"

I took a deep breath. "Coach, I want to play football for Red Bend this fall." I figured it'd be best to get it over with fast. Like pulling off a Band-Aid.

"Huh," he said, probably chewing his mustache right off but I was too busy studying the floor to see. "I thought you had some scholastic problems last semester."

Which, if you'd asked me the hundred things I thought he would say, wouldn't even have made the list. Also, how did he even know?

"Yeah," I said. "English."

"Because you need a clean transcript to play. You know that."

Which I did know but I guess I'd forgotten. "We're working on it, me and Mrs. Stolze." Which wasn't a complete lie because I'd talked to Mom about it once and gone through the file. "She said if I got her the papers I could turn it around."

"You need to work on that then, don't you?"

"Yeah. I guess I do."

"Okay then." Jeff turned to help a customer.

"But—Jeff? If I did that could I, you know, play?"

"I'll have to do some asking around. Don't know what the rules are." He turned away, smoothing his mustache, and started talking to a guy about subfloors, which would be fascinating if you had nothing else to think about for the rest of your life.

"Should I, you know, keep training?" I managed finally, sounding like a total moron I'm sure. The subfloor guy seemed to think I was, anyway.

"Oh, yeah. And say hey to your old man."

Yeah, right. It was Dad's fault I was in all this mess. Because you know what? I would never tell this to anyone, but all spring as the letters from Mrs. Stolze had kept coming home and I still wasn't doing anything and Mom was so upset, I just knew in my heart that it wasn't *that* serious. And maybe that was because I knew Dad had done the same thing. Maybe if I lived in a family where people got through school just on their grades and their brains and stuff, maybe I'd have cared more. Cared enough to pass, at least. Which I now had to do. So, not knowing where else to go, I headed over to Red Bend Elementary School to find Mom.

There were hardly any cars in the parking lot seeing as it

was the middle of summer, and the hallways had that echo schools have when there aren't any kids. There wasn't even a secretary. So I just stuck my head into the principal's office where I figured Mom would be and sure enough there she was, typing away on her computer.

"Hey," I said.

She jumped about three feet in the air. "Jesus, D.J.!"

"Oops. Guess I should have knocked."

"That's okay," she said, catching her breath.

The office sure looked different. There were lacy curtains and a windowsill full of plants, and some other plants in the corners, and pictures of us on the desk: the family portrait Mom made us do a couple years ago, my hair looking pretty much awful; Curtis as a little kid in a pile of footballs; me with my heifer Lee Roy Jordan and her first-place ribbon at the 4-H fair; and one I'd never seen before of Bill and a huge black guy in their Minnesota uniforms, standing side by side. It was framed and everything.

I picked it up. "Who's that?" I asked.

Mom took it away from me in that way moms have. "It's just something Bill sent me. That's his roommate, Aaron Johnson. He's from Detroit, he's a lineman—"

"Bill sent it to you?"

"He e-mailed it. I just printed it out," she shrugged like it wasn't anything, even though it was. "So," she asked, turning off her computer screen, "what's up?"

I felt like I was being sort of bombarded, like I'd walked in on her cheating or something, which now that I've given it more thought I guess she was. But at the moment I just sort of shoved it all aside and said instead, "I need to talk to Mrs. Stolze."

"Oh. English," Mom said. You could tell she was flustered. And then she rallied a little and gave me a big smile and said, "That's great, D.J. How can I help?"

"You could write the papers," I offered.

Mom gave me that hairy eyeball she can do and I grinned, and then we were back to being normal like nothing had happened.

"Well, Mary Stolze seemed awfully flexible when she talked to me," Mom continued. "She doesn't want you to miss basketball."

Which, stupid me, I hadn't even realized. I don't care about volleyball, and of course nobody knew about my football plans—and nobody except Jeff needed to, thank you very much, not until I knew for sure that I could play—but I was pretty important basketball-wise. Bill got through high school because he was a starter and he was getting a free college education too, and now that being-good-at-sports thing was rubbing off on me too. Finally.

"So I don't have to write anything?" I asked hopefully.

Mom gave me the eyeball again. "We'll work something out."

Which meant that I had to drive over to Mrs. Stolze's house, one of those houses I've always wanted with the garage under the bedrooms, and ring the doorbell and everything and talk to her.

But here's the super-weird thing: Jeff had already called her. So when I arrived she was acting like this was the most exciting thing that had ever happened to her. Now, Mrs. Stolze is a very nice lady and a great teacher, but she knows about as much about football as the heifers do. Less, probably, because at least they've been watching me and Brian. It's a huge joke all her classes have with her, how much she doesn't know.

"So what position are you playing?" she asked all nicely.

I had to cough so I wouldn't laugh, because I could have said something like Exterior Flame-Thrower and she would have believed me. But instead I said I wanted to be a running back, and she sat me down in her nice yellow kitchen and got me a pop and told me her idea. Which was pretty easy seeing as all it required was me working my guts out for the rest of the summer. And she promised not to tell anyone my football plan, like it was some huge military secret or something, and I said thank you very much for everything and I left.

As I drove home I guess I should have been thinking about how exactly I was going to spend the rest of the summer, what with preseason looming and everything, working my guts out for Mrs. Stolze. But instead all I could think about was Mom sitting there in her air-conditioned office with her lace curtains and her plants and her computer, and I'd bet our farm she was writing Win and Bill. That office, frankly, seemed more like a home than our house did. And she was there all the time too, from morning until dinner, and there wasn't anyone else in the building even, just her, and so how much could she get done working by herself? Besides writing e-mails and printing out Bill's pictures? Maybe that's all she did all day long when she wasn't looking for a real principal or doing other principal stuff.

It occurred to me, pulling into our driveway, that I wasn't the only person in our family keeping secrets.

19

THE OPPOSITE OF
FLIRTING

I didn't think about Mrs. Stolze's project for the rest of the
week either, if you want to know the truth, because there
was so much else going on. For one thing, thinking about
The Fight took up some time. Talking to Brian had brought
it all back, I guess you could say, and then finding out Mom
was writing Win and Bill for all these months without mentioning it, not even to *me*—well, it was a lot to think about.

And other things were changing too. It wasn't like Brian
and I were flirting or anything—it was the opposite of flirting, probably—but things were getting . . . different.

We were still running in the afternoons, which was nice
because we had a lot more wind now, and it wasn't so hard,
running down that country road. We'd always take our shirts
off because it was always so hot. Don't get the wrong idea—
it's not, you know, like a sports bra is revealing or anything.
At least it isn't on me. Besides, it's not fair that guys can go
around without their shirts whenever they feel like it but
girls have to stay all covered up like we're nuns or something.
Especially when it's as hot as it gets here in August.

So we ran along not talking too much, me keeping Brian going and him keeping me, and after a while a truck came up behind us, which doesn't happen too much where I live, and it slowed down a bit and then I heard:

"What the hell are you two doing?"

I jumped a foot. Dad was leaning out the passenger window as Curtis drove.

"Nothing." Which wasn't true because we were running, but I sounded guilty.

"You get some clothes on, you hear? I'm not running a goddam beach party."

I pulled out my T-shirt from my waistband, watching Dad adjust the rearview mirror so he could keep an eye on us, but then they drove over a hill and couldn't see us any more and I just tucked that T-shirt away and kept running. Brian didn't say anything and neither did I, but I could see out the corner of my eye he was grinning.

That night at dinner Mom kind of looked at me like there was something I wasn't telling her. Which there was, but I think what she thought I wasn't telling her was different from what I wasn't telling her actually. Anyway, I blushed.

Friday afternoon when we got back from running, Smut all thrilled to see us because we'd been half an hour and she'd started to panic, Brian asked what I was doing this weekend.

"I dunno. Work on an English paper, I guess."

Brian laughed. *"Romeo and Juliet* and all that?"

"Kind of. Remember back when all we had to do was draw a picture?"

"'My family.' With the blue line along the top for the sky." Brian grinned.

"Curtis used to draw these great pictures with the animal legs going in every direction like they'd been run over or something. Mom still has one on her dresser."

We grinned at that. Brian tossed me a water bottle from his trunk. "So that's what you're going to do? A picture of Romeo and Juliet and the tower and everything?"

"Yep," I said, dead serious. "All sixteen colors of crayon." And then, because it was just such a perfect moment, the light hitting Brian's face and his hair that's so shiny even though it's short, and the barn so pretty in the sunshine, I couldn't help it. I sprayed him full in the face with my water.

He let out a yell and came after me with a bottle in each hand, but I got to the hose in time and really blasted him, which would have been great except that once he was wet he didn't seem to care how much wetter he got and he started wrestling me for the hose so we both were soaking, and Smut was jumping everywhere and getting mud all over us, and then he got the hose away from me and his other arm around my waist so I couldn't get away and he just blasted me, and let me tell you the water was *cold*. It comes from our well and must be like fifty degrees and Brian must have been pretty mad because I couldn't get away even though I was re-ally wriggling and hollering and laughing hysterically—

And right then Amber drove up.

I froze.

Brian got me right in the face, but I wasn't playing any-more. He saw Amber and let go of me. "Who's that?"

"A friend of mine . . . Amber," I called, "this is Brian Nel-son."

"I know who he is," she said, leaning against Lori's Escort.

I turned the spigot off. Brian pulled a towel out of his trunk and started wiping off.

"So, I'll see you around?" I asked, wishing Amber would blink at least. I so wanted to say something else, ask if maybe he wanted to do something over the weekend. Not a date or anything like that, just something. But I couldn't. Even if Amber wasn't sitting right there watching us like we were some kind of laboratory experiment, her hair all orange and everything.

"Sure," he said. But he smiled at me as he pulled out. I think it was a smile.

I made a show out of getting my T-shirt on, wanting to keep that smile memory a bit. I didn't think Amber would be too pleased about Brian and me goofing off together like that.

"So," she asked, sauntering over, "are you two doing it yet?"

Nope. She wasn't pleased.

"Come on, Amber. We were just horsing around."

"For your information, guys like that don't go out with girls like you."

"I *know* that," I said, trying not to get mad.

"So you're thinking about it, then."

"Amber!" This is what she does. We don't argue much but when we do it really sucks. "It was hot, we were goofing off. Can we forget about it? Please?"

"Because you were all over him."

I tried to take a deep breath. "I was not."

"Now that I think about it, he probably would do it with you. But he'd tell everyone about it afterward, and they'd all laugh whenever they saw you."

"Shut up." Now I was mad.

"What, you think I'm not telling the truth?" she asked innocently.

"Just shut up."

"You're really hot for him, aren't you? That tight little butt and those strong arms? Is that why you never told me about him? Are you having sleepovers?"

"If you don't shut up, I'm going to punch you." I took a step toward her.

"Jeez, calm down already. Forget about it. Let's go out."

"Uh-uh." I walked toward the house.

"Come on. We'll go to the movies or something. I've got beer."

"Go to hell." I didn't even turn around.

"Jeez. I'm sorry."

But there was no way on earth I was getting into that car. Not without strangling her first. I slammed the door behind me. After a while I heard her car start up so I guess she drove away. With her beer.

Boy oh boy, was I mad. I was so mad that if I'd been a different sort of person I'd have kicked Smut or punched Curtis, which neither of them deserved, plus Curtis would punch me back. I ended up in the hayloft punching the hay bales instead, which cut my hands all up and got me over being mad pretty fast.

So then I just sat there ripping up hayseeds and thinking what a jerk Amber was. About how she made fun of everyone in the world but no one could make fun of her, how she didn't know anything about boys anyway because she'd never even had a boyfriend, not counting this kid Andy she used to arm-wrestle until he moved away.

Not that I'm the world's biggest expert on boys—which is probably clear seeing as I've written a million pages already and haven't mentioned them at all in that way—but at least I've gone out with a couple. Well, one. If you call seeing a movie your freshman year with your big brother and his girlfriend and his friend Troy Lundstrom "going out." But Troy, well, it's not like our family is a bunch of rocket scientists or anything, but we are compared to him.

Then last year I didn't really hang out with anyone, especially after quitting basketball. I didn't even go to the prom because Amber didn't want to go with any guys from Red Bend and besides I didn't have a dress or anything, so instead we hung out in my room with a bottle of schnapps she'd stolen from work and we drank it all and I threw up, and I had to get up the next morning to milk and I threw up again in the manure gutter, and if I live my entire life without seeing another bottle of schnapps, that would be absolutely fine with me.

So I just want to make it clear that it's not like I don't like guys. I do. And I've had a boyfriend if that's what you want to call Troy Lundstrom, for a couple hours at least. But I didn't have one at the present moment. And I wished someone like Brian's Oprah mom who was good at asking questions would ask Amber why she needed to be such a jerk and say all these things just to make me mad and hurt my feelings.

But then what would I say back? Why did the things she'd said hurt so much? Because it's not like Amber hasn't talked like that a million times before, and most of the time it makes me laugh. If she'd said it about Brian a week before, it probably wouldn't have bothered me at all. I probably would have agreed with her, even. Guys like Brian, they don't go for girls' basketball starters who also know about dairy farming. They go for cute short girls with lots of hair and lots of makeup and long fingernails, and there's absolutely not one thing on that list that applies to me. So why did it make me so mad now?

Because I guess I pretty much liked Brian. I sure didn't want to think about it if you haven't noticed, but I liked him a lot. I liked being around him. I had friends in school and I had Amber, but I'd never felt this way before, of wanting to be with someone all the time, and talk to him, and run with him in my sports bra. I didn't mind that last part one bit.

But Brian, as Amber explained, wasn't for me. Girls like me dated tackles and guards, guys who probably lettered but wouldn't get scholarships, and would go to local colleges maybe and end up working in hardware stores. And you know, I've never minded that. I was okay with that because I'd lived with a couple star players and watched girls climb all over them and I didn't like those girls at all.

But now it made me sick to my stomach, the thought that I was one of those girls too. But I didn't like Brian because he was a quarterback, I liked him even though he was a quarterback. Which is a big difference that no one would understand but me. Certainly not Amber. She could make fun of Brian all she wanted, but I'd had more conversations with him, real conversations about real subjects, in one week than I'd had with Amber in all the time we've been friends. At least with Brian I was thinking about feelings, not just my feelings but other people's feelings too, which Amber never does.

Anyway, now I was stuck home on Friday night with no one to talk to but Smut. And figuring out all this stuff about Brian, about how I felt and everything, just made me feel ten times worse. All that padding I had around me from my great idea to play football was gone. So much had happened over the week, all these revelations and lies and talks and workouts and hair problems, all this liking-Brian business, that it had just worn away. And right now I really needed some of that padding back.

20

THE MOST DISGUSTING THING
I'VE EVER HEARD OF

Saturday was about the most fun anyone has ever had in the history of the world. Listening to Jeff Peterson talk about subflooring would be a trip to Disney World in comparison. I milked, of course, and did some work around the barn, and tried not to think about Brian, which was like trying not to breathe. Finally I couldn't stand it anymore and went to see Kari at Jorgensen's Ice Cream. She was really busy but she gave me a big smile, which cheered me up a lot, and invited me to a party at the gravel pit, which cheered me up even more.

So after milking I took a long shower and tried to figure out what to do with my hair, and ended up with a ponytail again—someone out there has all the hairstyling brains I should have been born with—and a clean pair of jeans and a Red Bend T-shirt, so you can see how totally sexy I was, and went off in Mom's Caravan as she yelled "drive safely" after me because if she didn't the police will come and arrest her and put her in prison. That's what she told me, anyhow.

The party turned out to be pretty big, with kegs and a bunch of teen counselors from local summer camps. I don't go to many parties like this, which probably doesn't surprise you too much, and I'm not much of a drinker, but it was nice anyway. I talked a bit with Kari's brother Kyle, who's Red Bend's starting QB and who said it was too bad Curtis couldn't play for Red Bend because it would be really nice to have a Schwenk on the team. That was weird. Then his girlfriend came over and didn't want to talk football, so they went somewhere else.

Brian wasn't there.

I ended up sitting on an old log with Kari, looking over all those people talking and having fun. Kari chattered away for a while but then she got quiet too.

I sighed this huge sigh, feeling just so miserable. "Can I ask you something?"

"Sure, D.J.," she said, looking ready for some big conversation.

"What's your favorite ice cream flavor?"

She broke up like it was the funniest thing she'd ever heard. It might have been the beer. It cheered me up too, if you want to know the truth. We laughed pretty hard.

Just then Amber of all people showed up, nodding to me like we hadn't had a huge fight the day before. The three of us sat there not saying too much. All of a sudden I asked, "Can you two keep a secret?"

"It depends." Kari grinned.

"Uh-huh," Amber said, not taking her eyes off me, and I knew she was thinking about Brian.

I dug at the log, peeling the bark off.

"What is it?" Kari asked, nudging me. "Come on. My lips are sealed."

"Your lips are covered in beer," I said, which made her giggle.

There was this long silence again. I guess I could have said forget it and walked away and that would have been the end of it. But I don't think that fast. If I thought that fast I wouldn't have opened up my mouth in the first place.

"It's just—please, don't tell anyone—I'm going to try out for the football team."

"Jesus," Amber said.

I kept working away at that log. "Jeff Peterson is finding out if it's even possible . . . Please don't tell Kyle." I already regretted opening my mouth. If he found out, or anyone, and it turned out I couldn't . . . that would be the worst. Finally I looked at Kari.

She was grinning the biggest grin I've ever seen. "Then I'm doing cheerleading."

"What!" Amber and I both gasped.

"Why not? If you've got the guts for football, I can at least do that. Volleyball sucks! I'll get to wear a little uniform, do all those dance steps—I used to do gymnastics, you know."

"But you—come on, Kari—" I couldn't even speak.

"Besides, you need someone to cheer you on."

I couldn't believe it. I mean, football is one thing. But cheerleading? I'd never have the guts to do that. Although Kari could really yell during basketball, and she liked people.

She grinned at me again. "Don't back out on me now."

"No way." I turned to Amber. "So what do you think? You in?"

Amber took a swig of beer. "I think it's stupid and pathetic."

We both laughed for a second until we realized she was serious.

"You're just playing football so you can be around all those guys."

"No, I'm not—" I said.

"It's disgusting. It's the most disgusting thing I've ever heard of." She drained her beer. "You seriously need to reexamine your priorities." And she stomped off, just like that.

Well. Kari and I sat there for a few minutes, feeling pretty squashed.

"What's up with her?" Kari asked.

I had no idea. "I hope she doesn't tell anyone."

"Who'd she tell? We're the only people she talks to." Kari had a point.

"Do you think it's disgusting?" I had to ask.

"I think it's totally cool, and I think you're going to kick their asses, and I think you're going to be twice as good as your brothers."

"No way," I said. But I didn't say it too loudly. I wanted those words to, you know, stay in the air a bit longer. Then Kyle came by, and Kari just kept going on and on about football and how Red Bend was missing a couple key players that the team could not live without, until eventually I had to give her a nudge but unfortunately I nudged her just as she was drinking so she ended up with beer down her shirt, which she didn't seem to mind but I felt bad. Anyway, it was about time for me to leave.

When I got to Mom's Caravan, there was Amber sitting on the hood, which is hard to do because it slopes so much. She looked like she'd been there awhile.

"Hey," I said. "You okay?"

She nodded, studying her beer cup.

"You sure?" I asked finally, just for something to say.

"You really like him, don't you?" she asked, more to the cup than to me.

I shrugged. "You're right. He'd never go out with me."

"Do you like him?" she asked again.

I nodded. It was too much to say out loud.

"Do you, you know, fool around with him?"

I shook my head. Even thinking about that made me hurt.

Amber studied her beer. "You don't get it, do you?"

"I told you, it would never happen—"

"You're with me."

"I'm—what?"

"You're with me. You're not with him. It's the two of us. Don't you see that?"

All of a sudden I could barely stand. And it wasn't the beer, I can assure you.

"Say something," she said.

I swallowed hard. "I don't know what to—I didn't know. I didn't know that."

"How could you not know?" Amber asked miserably.

"How . . . how long have you known?"

"Years. I've known for years."

Remember when I said that I only saw Amber cry one time, when Hawley beat us in basketball? Well, I lied. Because I could see tears on her face now, in the moonlight.

"I'm sorry." That's all I could think of to say. It was so totally lame.

Amber slid off the Caravan and walked away. She didn't look back, and I didn't follow her.

So. That gave me a little something to think about driving home. Amber was . . . one of those people. Jeez. I don't say "those people" like it's a bad thing. But those words—*lesbian, homosexual, gay*—they're like medical words. Like *cancer*. I didn't want to think of Amber having cancer. I know, you die from cancer and you don't die from being gay, not unless you have AIDS, which I've never heard of anyone in Wisconsin having. I know I sound like a stupid hick moron, but I bet it would be a shock to you too, if you found out your best friend was in love with you and thought of the two of you as some sort of couple without you even having a single clue. Which I guess really does make me a moron.

But really, when you think about it, it explained a lot. Like why Amber never had a boyfriend. Or why she was so happy to drive me around and buy my movie tickets. And drink beer with me in her mom's car. And skip the prom so we could get drunk together and sleep over. And give me back rubs whenever I needed them . . . The more I thought about it, the more weirded out I got until I wanted to stop somewhere and wash my hands or something. But as mad as I was at myself for never seeing it, never seeing how she always made jokes about people being gay because of course she was gay herself, I was just as mad that she'd never told me. Because if nothing else, I'd have told her that even though it didn't look like it, I really like guys. Which is why I guess she never told me, because she's not dumb.

Lying in bed that night, I had to laugh out loud. Here I was stupid in love with a boy who'd never even look twice in my direction while my best friend was stupid in love with me. If I didn't laugh, I would have started crying.

There's another thing too, which is probably none of my business and I probably sound really stupid even saying it, but it's something I've been trying to figure out ever since Mom had to explain what those words meant and why there were some people who acted that way and all. But you know how on TV shows the guys who are really into guys go into fashion or hairdressing or dancing or something like that? It seems to me that if you're a guy who really likes guys, you should do something like, well, like football. Because football is as much about guys as anything I could think of. Not counting me, anyway. And the opposite too, that whole thing about tough women being into guy things? Sometimes Amber and I get called names when we play basketball, which I guess is right on the money for one of us at least. But don't you think girls who really liked girls would go for fashion and hairdressing instead? Not basketball. Because I look at the cute girls in our school, the ones with makeup and pink clothes and blow dryers, and I can really see why guys like that. Not that I want to go out with those girls or anything, but I get it. Get it enough to see how I don't measure up. Amber's been my best friend for six years, and I'm sorry but I've never once thought she was hot. Which I guess is part of our whole miscommunication thing.

So anyway, I just wanted to give that huge long speech to explain the look I give people when they say mean stuff about me being on the team. I don't say anything back, of course. But I think to myself that if I was a lesbian I wouldn't be playing football. I'd be working checkout at the Super Saver.

21

WHO EVER SAID LOVE WAS FUN?

$\mathcal{I}$ woke up Sunday morning totally fried. I think my poor little brain had blown a couple fuses trying to figure out me and Amber, not to mention me and Brian, and me and Curtis, and me and Dad. And me and Mom . . . looking back, I'm surprised smoke wasn't coming out of my ears or something from all that thinking.

What was I going to do about Amber? I didn't even want to think about her. It was too much. I didn't want to think about Brian either, but even though I hated it I couldn't get him off my mind. It hurt to think about him. It physically hurt. You know those eight million songs they play on the radio about how great it is to be in love and how it feels like walking on clouds or something? Let me tell you: those songs are wrong.

And it hurt too—especially because Amber pointed it out—that now I was one of those girls who hang around football players like flies on flypaper. Like they did around Win, calling even though he wasn't interested much and even on dates he'd only talk about football, but the girls hung on every word he said, like he was some sort of genius. Even the smart girls, the girls who got good grades and were going to college. I hate it whenever anyone makes a crack about stupid girls, and I gave Justin Hunsberger a black eye, a really good one, in fourth grade when he called me that once. But when I saw those girls hanging all over Win, I really had to wonder. Especially because Win's skin was sort of bad and he wasn't so handsome anyway, not like Bill, who always had girlfriends and who Dad once caught in the barn with a girl doing what I think you can imagine.

So thinking about all this stuff was the extent of my thrilling weekend, and Monday Brian came back. Which should have made me really happy, but I felt so jangled up, what with all those blown brain fuses, that seeing him, having him so close, made it that much worse.

"Hey there," he said, starting right away on the weights.

"Hey," I said, shoveling cow poop. Then every single possible other thing I could have said just went right out my mind, like I was a TV that someone turned off.

"How was your weekend?" he asked.

"Great." And then, because this was the biggest lie ever told in the history of the world, and because I could never tell Brian one bit of the truth, I had to laugh.

"Yours too, huh?" he asked, grinning.

And you know? That made me feel a million times better,

and the hurt of seeing him, and the brain fuse pain, all of that sort of faded away for a while.

"What, did your house burn down or something?" I asked.

"Nah." He shrugged. "It's nothing. Me and my girlfriend broke up is all."

"Oh." That was interesting. *Really* interesting. "I'm sorry," I managed to get out finally.

"It's no big deal."

I couldn't help wondering if maybe it had something to do with me, like our water fight and all. But then I realized that I was totally stupid and there's no way it could *ever* be about me, not in a million years, not if I was the only girl on the entire planet. Then after a long time I thought that maybe I should say something Oprah-like, ask him if he wanted to talk about it. But by that point I'd wasted so much time that I couldn't. It would just sound stupid. And it hit me that this was just like The Fight during Christmas, where there was this opportunity when someone could have said something but didn't and now it was too late forever.

So I finished with the poop and we fed the calves and cleaned up the milking equipment and painted the barn, waiting for Dad and Curtis to take off. Finally they did and we headed out to the heifer field. We had a good workout and it felt great to pound on my body, forget all those brain issues for a while. Although I was really careful not to get too close to Brian, because whenever I did I started hurting again, and if nothing else it's hard to play football when all you can think about is how much you hurt. But sometimes we'd bump into each other by accident and, well, it was hard for me to figure out which was stronger—the pain or, for that one second our shoulders touched, how good I felt.

It just got worse from there. For example, Tuesday morning Brian was doing sit-ups on this cruddy old blanket he uses, and I was feeding the calves and didn't have anything else to do, so without even thinking about it I came over and locked my ankles with his and started doing sit-ups with him. Which if you've ever done a sport you know that you do every day of practice. Anyway, it got to be a contest between us and even though we both knew Brian would win, I was really working at it and so was he, until my gut hurt so bad and I was panting and blowing, trying to keep up, and he was panting and blowing, trying to keep ahead of me, and right then Dad stomped up. We hadn't even heard him come in, I guess because we were making so much noise.

"What the hell is going on!" he snarled, looking as mad as I'd ever seen him.

Brian and I looked at each other and in one second figured out what Dad must have been thinking as he heard us puffing away, and—you know how if you turn two magnets backwards you can't stick them together again? That's how Brian and I reacted. We leapt right up off the floor.

"Sit-ups," Brian managed to get out. "Sir."

And frankly, we were. I mean, it's really hard for two people to fool around if only their ankles are touching. People I know, anyway.

"Sit-ups!" Dad glared at us.

"You know." I gulped. "Training."

Dad snorted. He eyed Brian. "You up to speed on milking yet?"

Oh. I'd forgotten all about it—and I bet you did too—but remember back when Mom asked me to drive Curtis to Madison for the Little League awards banquet? Well, if you recall I had not been the happiest person about it. But just because I stomped out and didn't come back and had to eat mailbox tomatoes, that didn't stop them for one second from assuming that I would still do it and Brian and Dad would milk Thursday night and Friday morning.

"Pretty much," I lied.

"You make sure he knows what he's doing," Dad said, looking us both over. The fact that the calves were kicking the empty milk buckets everywhere didn't help the situation.

So he hung around watching us clean up, which would have been bad enough in any situation, but that whole business of him thinking that we'd been fooling around made it ten times worse. Also, Brian really didn't know much about cleaning up after milking because of course he spent most of the cleanup time on his training. So I had to explain everything to him with Dad watching us and me having trouble because Brian was so close I could smell his shampoo and his mom's detergent in his clothes, and it wasn't that they smelled bad at all, but they just got in the way of my breathing for a while.

That afternoon when we were running, I kept my shirt on.

"Jeez," Brian said, "I thought your dad was just about going to kill me."

"Kill both of us."

We could laugh about it, now that it was over and everything.

I grinned. "He caught Bill in the barn once."

"No way! Who with?"

"Christine Petrosky."

"Who's she?"

"She was a senior. It was Bill's freshman year, and he was—"

"Your brother was messing around with a senior?" Brian was impressed.

"Oh, yeah. And Dad started hollering so we all ran out thinking the barn was on fire, and there they were all embarrassed, and Win got all mad because it was during football season and he didn't want Bill tiring himself out—"

"You're kidding."

"Mom tried to hustle me and Curtis back inside so we

wouldn't see what was going on, like it wasn't completely obvious." I laughed — we both laughed — thinking about this.

"So what'd your dad do?"

"What could he do? It was the middle of the season. Bill was a starter already. I don't know what he did. No one really talked about it much."

"With a senior. Jeez." Brian was still impressed.

"Yeah. She was real pretty too."

"A senior."

We ran along for a bit thinking about that, and after a while it just really bummed me out, the thought of Bill getting all those girls so easily and me not able to get one guy. I don't know what Brian was thinking, but out of the blue he asked about the trip Curtis and me were taking to Madison and started talking about how cool Madison was, how he'd been there lots of times for football games, and normally it would have depressed me to pieces, but instead thanks to Amber I got an idea. A very good idea.

Not that I had any chance to thank her. Tuesday night I had to drive Curtis to a friend's house, and as I was leaving Dad handed me a grocery list of stuff he needed. Which meant I'd have to go into the Super Saver where Amber worked. I was still pretty shook up from our big conversation on Saturday night and not too sure I even wanted to see her, but it's not like when you're shopping for groceries in Red Bend you have much choice of stores.

The minute I went in, I spotted her—you could be legally blind and still see her with that orange hair she had—but I pretended I didn't. I mean, I was going to say hey to her once I was checking out, but it's pretty weird to get all friendly with the checkout people when you just walk in. I think it is, anyway. Amber didn't say anything to me either. I'd say that she didn't see me, but she didn't see me so much that it was pretty clear she wasn't seeing me on purpose.

I wandered around trying to get all Dad's stuff, which turned out to be like one of those TV shows with the obstacle course and the map and this was the final episode. Here's what was on the list: peppercorns, fresh parsley, and lard. I didn't even know they *made* lard. I thought it was some old-fashioned thing, like quill pens. I spent about an hour in the produce section trying to figure out which pile of green stuff was parsley, and finally I had to ask someone about the other two and it took that guy another hour to find lard and he *works* there, and then finally I had peppercorns and a box with LARD in big letters on the side, like they were proud of it or something.

So I headed over to the checkout part but Amber wasn't at her register—another girl was there. I even asked where Amber was and the girl said, all bored, "She went on break. She's not supposed to go on break now but she said it was an emergency."

Well. It was pretty clear that Amber didn't want to talk to me, and I sure wasn't going to poke around out back behind the Super Saver looking for her. So I just went home with my lard, feeling relieved if you want to know the truth, and a little smug too because at least I'd meant to talk to her when I was ready, and once I was home I just tried to get ready for the big trip to Madison.

All week Mom grilled me on it, how to get there and where to stay and where the banquet was even though I knew it pretty much already, and I have to say I didn't give much more thought to Amber. Mom got us reservations in a dorm with a bunch of other families coming in for the banquet, and she gave me money for breakfast and gas, and emergency money just in case. Plus I had to make sure Brian was up to speed on the milking so Dad didn't think we were idiots, which meant a lot of time showing him how to clean the cows' udders and hook up the milk machine and then clean them up all over again when they're done, the cows all irritated and thwacking both of us in the head the whole time with their tails, although I at least was way too preoccupied to notice.

Wednesday afternoon Dad and Curtis went to another PT appointment so Brian and I had a couple hours to work out. We were both in a really good mood. We only had one more workout after this, on Friday afternoon, because preseason started on Monday. I was feeling so fit and psyched and everything, and Brian was too, that we did a whole bunch of tackling drills. Every time I'd come after Brian it took the sting out of things a little more, if that makes any sense. I knew I wasn't cool enough to go out with him ever, or hang out or anything, but at least I could knock him down. It makes me sound like I'm four years old or something. Most of the time I probably am.

Then after some running drills we were so beat that I flopped down right there on the field and looked up at the clouds in the sky making those weird faces they always make.

"Oof," said Brian, falling down next to me. "I am ready to rule preseason."

"I'm ready for my legs to fall off," I said, and we both laughed.

"I really want to thank you for all this," he said.

"What, the football field? Think I could be an NFL groundskeeper?" I grinned.

"I'm serious. For training me. And for talking. It's been real important."

"Don't worry about it." I grinned again. I mean, what else could I say?

We lay there for a bit, listening to the birds and everything, and it was just really nice and peaceful. After a while I started dozing I think because I was so beat. I could hear Brian next to me, rustling. Then—I hate to write this, just thinking about it makes my hands sweat, it was absolutely the most horrible moment of my life—

He kissed me.

That part wasn't horrible. It wasn't—well, in the movies they make it out to be nice and soft, and the music starts and birds sing and two people gaze into each other's eyes. The problem is the movies never show how you're supposed to *warn* someone before you do that. You don't just lean over and do that right out of the blue to someone who has their eyes closed.

It would have been nice, it really would have been, if I'd had just a second to enjoy it. Just a second to think to myself that Brian had his lips on mine and he was kissing me in a really romantic way that was better than anything I'd ever let myself hope for. And someday, maybe, if I'm reincarnated or something because nothing that nice will ever happen to me again as long as I live, I'll be in that situation again and I'll handle it right. Or maybe the guy will warn me.

Because Brian didn't warn me, and I felt this thing and sat up with a jerk and smacked my head into his nose and he started bleeding. That was the horrible part.

And I won't go into any more detail except to say that I apologized at least ten thousand times and ran around trying to find him cold water because God knows there wasn't any ice up there in that field, and we ended up using his T-shirt to stop the bleeding, which probably wasn't the best thing to ever happen to his T-shirt in the history of the world, and eventually he could laugh about it but I couldn't. And this probably won't surprise you, but we didn't once for the rest of the day try kissing again.

When he left that afternoon, he was still making little jokes that were probably funny but just cut through me like knives. We didn't run, which probably doesn't surprise you either. I just walked him to his car with his T-shirt all wadded up to hide the bloody part, and his face didn't look that bad either, all things considered. We'd washed the blood off.

"I'm real sorry," I said for the 10,001st time.

"It's okay. I can barely feel it. I think you snapped a nerve or something." I must have looked so awful that he added really fast, "I'm kidding."

I nodded miserably.

He climbed into the Cherokee. "Hey. Cheer up, okay?"

I nodded again.

"So I'll see you Friday afternoon? One last workout?" And he, well, he touched my hand a little bit. Not much, but enough. Enough for me to think that maybe I could just live through the trip to Madison and everything, long enough to make it to Friday.

22

THE BANQUET

So the next morning, right after milking and breakfast, we set off for Madison. If you ever have to drive anywhere for five hours and you're sitting by yourself or with my brother Curtis, which is basically the same thing, and you're looking for topics to think about to pass the time, I have a few to suggest:

1. You're crazy in love with a guy who's way too cute and popular and smart for you, and you'd do almost anything to get close to him, and then when out of the blue he tells you he's just broken up with his girlfriend and kisses you, you break his nose. Well, I didn't break it technically, but that doesn't matter. Every time I thought about what had happened I'd blush deep red. Then eventually I got to the point where I didn't blush, I'd just feel like throwing up. Because even if his breakup did have something to do with me — which was impossible to believe except for that kissing part — there sure wasn't any way it would matter anymore.

2. You find out that for the past few years you've been dat-

ing your best friend without even realizing it. That in and of itself could cover an hour or two. Jeepers. That image of Amber crying on the hood of the Caravan — I won't be forgetting that anytime soon. I'd never had a conversation, a real conversation, with her until Saturday night because, I realized now, any conversation would probably lead right to the Big One. About you-know-what. And if Amber couldn't talk to me about that, well then, I guess she figured she couldn't talk to me about anything. I'll tell you one thing: I sure didn't feel like talking to her now. I had this horrible fear that she'd find out somehow, she'd dig it out of me the way she does, what happened between Brian and me kissing and all, and then she would never for the rest of my life let me forget it. If she was going to take off whenever I showed up, that was A-okay with D.J. Schwenk.

3. You try to figure out what it will be like playing football — if I could even play football, seeing as Jeff Peterson hadn't yet told me yes — with thirty-odd boys who probably aren't altogether happy with the notion of having a girl on their team. And even if I didn't make the team, I still had a couple days to get through before cuts. I'm pretty tough, but it can get ugly out there sometimes. Ask anyone who's ever played football. Like my two brothers, who have stories that would chill your blood. Or Dad, who lost his teeth, and his hip eventually, playing tackle.

4. You've decided that you really have to cut off your hair,

which is hard enough, but now you have to figure out how. Amber — my old friend Amber, not the new stranger Amber I didn't like thinking about — read once that if you want a good haircut, ask someone whose haircut you like where they got it done. So, if you want to know the absolute truth, that was the big brilliant idea I'd had, to go to Madison and do exactly that. The only hitch was that it involved a) actually asking someone, which isn't one of my greatest skills, and b) actually going into some hair salon, which I'd never done in my life unless you count Amber's living room. So worrying about that took a couple hours and also left me feeling pretty sick to my stomach.

5. You have a little brother who may or may not be afraid to talk, but of course you can't talk about it because that would involve talking. I didn't even get to that one until we started seeing signs for Madison.

"How do you feel?" I asked Curtis.

He jumped, and shrugged.

"Are you nervous?" I asked.

He kind of shook his head.

Wow. That sure was a heartfelt conversation.

So I dropped him off at some baseball field so he could take part in an exhibition game for charity or something. I was supposed to stay and watch, but instead I took every ounce of strength I had and drove around until I found a street that obviously cool people used because it had bookstores and bike racks, and I parked our cruddy old Caravan and went into a coffee shop, feeling about as comfortable as a gorilla, staring at everyone out of the corner of my eye until they probably thought I was there to rob them or something. The coffee was good, though. And I had a brownie, but I've got to admit it wasn't as good as Dad's.

Finally, because I didn't have all week or anything, I sidled up to this girl, and I guess I kind of scared her until I could get out that I liked her hair and where did she get it cut. She was really nice about it in the end. She even drew a little map on a napkin because I was so nervous I was having trouble concentrating.

I got to the place and stood outside for a while, screwing up my courage to go in. You're probably laughing reading this, and I guess you have a right to laugh because it is kind of funny. Here I was all ready to try out for football, a sport where people get their legs broken, or their necks sometimes, and yet I couldn't walk into this one little beauty salon.

But finally I did, and I guess I should stop talking about how awful it was, but it was pretty awful, like when they asked if I had an appointment, which I didn't but the girl with the jewelry in her nose said they could take me anyway, and then the shampoo girl had to keep telling me what to do, like how I had to lie back and stuff, and when she asked where I was from I blushed because I might as well have had "farm hick" on my forehead. At about ten different points I would have walked right out but I didn't think fast enough, and then once I had shampoo in my hair I couldn't.

I ended up sitting in front of a mirror with all my wet hair, staring at my reflection and wondering if anyone that bad-looking had ever been in this chair before, while a girl named Mica, which she pronounced Meeka, which is good because who wants to be named after a rock, tugged a comb through. "So what do you want?" she asked.

"Um, a haircut?" I managed to get out.

She smirked kind of. "That's good . . . Just a trim?"

"I need it short. Because . . ." What did I have to lose, telling the truth? "The ponytail rubs against the football helmet."

Mica/Meeka eyed me. "You play football?"

"I'm, um, trying out."

"Your school has a girls' football team?"

I shook my head, which was dumb because she was combing my hair. "It's the boys' team," I said, kind of quiet.

Mica studied me in the mirror. "You're kidding."

I shook my head again.

"Anyone doing that," she said like she was saying it to herself, "needs to look good."

And I did in the end. She cut off a whole bunch of hair so it was sort of near my ears but in a really nice not-boy way, and she did this amazing thing using my cowlick so the hair came down around my face in this way that looked not very much at all like Red Bend and a lot like New York City. But in a good way that kind of showed off the little brown freckles on my nose, which before this I'd never thought were worth showing off.

I was really pleased. You could tell because I couldn't stop smiling, and I kept looking at my reflection in the mirrors that were everywhere. Mica liked it too, and walked me up to the front desk and made a big deal about getting my name and address even though I wasn't going to be driving back for a trim anytime soon.

There was this really cute guy standing next to me paying for his haircut. When he heard my name he asked if I was any relation to Bill Schwenk who played for Minnesota.

"He's my brother," I said, even though it was hard to talk because this guy was so cute I couldn't really look at him.

"Well," Mica added, "she plays on the boys' team at her high school."

"Really?" the cute guy said, looking at me so much I couldn't breathe. "That would be something to see." And he smiled a big smile at me and walked out.

And that smile kept me going for the next couple hours. It got me through the price of the haircut, which the girl at the front desk said like she said it all the time, which I guess she does, and which basically equaled the price of our dorm room *and* breakfast but which I paid because, well, I didn't have a choice and also, I told myself later, because the haircut was so good it was almost worth it. His smile got me through the awards banquet, which was just as boring as you can imagine, so boring I fell asleep, which was good because we were going to have to drive home that night seeing as I'd spent all our money.

So after the banquet I piled Curtis into the car and off we went. "Did you have fun?" I asked once, just to make conversation.

Curtis shrugged. He'd won an MVP award. The speaker kept joking about how big he is, which he hates but, well, it's hard not to notice. So we rode along, me drinking coffee and thinking about everything that had happened. Wondering if Brian would like my haircut.

"Why'd you cut your hair?" Curtis asked. In the silence it was like a gunshot.

I thought about what to say. One nice thing about talking to Curtis is that there's never any pressure for, you know, a quick response. You can mull it over. I decided what the heck. He was going to find out anyway.

"Because I'm going out for football," I said.

"Oh." He went back to looking out his window.

We rode along for another couple hundred years, me thinking that it really was good that I told him because it sure gave us something to talk about—

"Does Dad know?" he asked.

"No!" I said it sharper than I'd meant to. I couldn't help it.

Curtis kept looking out his window. I thought about all the things I could say right now, explaining why I was doing it, or why I didn't want Dad to know, or at least that we were driving home because I'd spent all Mom's money on my hair. But it wouldn't have mattered because Curtis, well, who knew what he was thinking because he sure wouldn't say anything back. And all of sudden this really bummed me out. And I started thinking about what Brian had said about Curtis being afraid to talk.

I thought about this for a long time. And it occurred to me all of sudden that maybe, well, maybe it had something to do with football. For Curtis, just like it did for me. I was all excited about playing football because it was something I wasn't supposed to do. Well, Curtis was *supposed* to do it. How many times had we heard that Curtis was bigger than Bill at his age, or that he had a great arm, or how tough he was? He'd been playing football with us since he could walk, which was early. He split his eyebrow open tackling Bill once and Win carried him home, both of them covered in blood, telling him the whole time what a great football player he was, and he had to go to the ER and get eight stitches. But maybe Curtis had the same sort of really complicated feelings about football that I had. God knows I couldn't talk about how I felt; I couldn't even imagine Curtis trying to.

"You know," I said, the noise startling both of us, "you don't have to play."

Curtis turned to look at me.

"Just because Win plays football, and Bill, and me if I make the team, that doesn't mean you have to."

Curtis frowned, suspicious.

"I'm serious. You don't have to do anything you don't want to do, you know."

Curtis studied his hands, and his new pants that Mom had bought him for the trip.

"I'm just playing because it's, you know, something different," I explained. "And because it'll give Dad a heart attack." Which got him to grin.

"I'm good at it," he said, really quiet.

"So what? I'm good at flunking English but I don't plan to make a career out of it."

That made us both smile too.

"What do you really want to do?" I asked.

Curtis studied his hands a lot more. "You'll laugh. It's stupid."

"It can't be that stupid. What?"

Long, long silence.

"Come on. I'm your sister. Please?"

Curtis sighed again. He looked out the window at the trees flashing past in the night, the lights of a mall glowing somewhere in the distance. In the tiniest voice you ever heard, he said, "I want to be a dentist."

I burst out laughing. And then I saw his face and realized

like a slap that he was serious. And in that split second his face clamped down and I realized I would never, ever get him to talk to me again.

Boy oh boy, did that make me mad. Because if you're going to go around saying you want to be a dentist, you've got to warn people. You don't just say it right out. If he'd said he wanted to be a tap dancer, it wouldn't have surprised me as much. Because that at least is physical. Those guys are jocks at least in their own way.

So we drove along for another hundred years, not saying anything. I was so mad at him for making me laugh like that. And then I started having these thoughts, these little thoughts that came into my brain against my will, like he did warn me and I promised to take him seriously and it kind of was my fault. And I started thinking that this was just like what happened between Dad and Win and Bill and me, how someone said something mean and everyone just sort of froze in their angry mode, and seven months later we're still like that and we might be like that forever.

Well, I didn't like thinking about that too much, so I started thinking instead about what Curtis had said. Now that I thought about it, it kind of made sense, him wanting to be a dentist. Because he always liked going to the dentist, and he takes really good care of his teeth and other people's teeth too, like Dad's false teeth. And he had all those skulls. It wasn't because they were *skulls*, I figured out like a bolt of lightning: it was because he liked to see the teeth fitted to-gether. Now that I had time to really analyze it, in fact, I was kind of surprised I hadn't figured this out earlier because it was so obvious. Kind of like Amber and me. But I sure didn't want to think about *that*.

And then I started thinking about what Brian's mom would say about all this, her being Oprah Winfrey and all. And it got to be a little conversation I was having with Oprah just like she was sitting there in the Caravan right behind me.

"Do you think you should apologize to Curtis?" Oprah asked.

"You know our family. We never apologize."

"Do you think that's a good thing?"

I didn't answer.

"I think you need to say something to your brother," she said gently.

I thought it over. Brian apologized to me once and it didn't kill him. It almost had but not quite. But he probably had a lot of experience, with his mom and all.

"Is this how you want to live your life?" Oprah asked, just to jab me a little.

I sighed. "Curtis?" I said.

He didn't respond in one single way.

"Curtis, I'm real sorry I laughed. That was a real awful thing for me to do."

He nodded just the tiniest bit.

"I won't laugh about it anymore. I promise."

We rode in silence for a while. The more I thought about Curtis as a dentist, the more used to it I got. After a while, Oprah left. Maybe she changed the channel.

"You know," I said, "I heard once about sports dentists. You could get a job with a hockey team or a football team just taking care of players' teeth. That would be cool."

Curtis went back to studying his hands. "I like how Dr. Wilson is so nice to all the kids. Even the scared ones. He lets them touch his tools and stuff, gets them used to it so they're not scared. I always like watching him do that."

Not only was this the longest thing I'd ever heard Curtis say, it was also the nicest.

"Yeah," I said. "That's pretty great."

"I was thinking next year about working at a camp maybe. Because little kids, they talk so much, they don't care if you don't."

I squeezed his shoulder. "You say everything you need to say."

That made him smile.

After a while I was low on gas so we stopped at a truck stop and while we were there had dinner, a second dinner, and it was *so* much better than the banquet food. I spent the rest of Mom's money on burgers and milk shakes and sundaes too, and Curtis probably would have had a second sundae but I wanted to get back on the road. We didn't say too much but I did kid him a little about him being so tall at the banquet, which he didn't seem to mind, and then out of the blue he asked if I was going out for quarterback, which made us just fall down laughing. And then when we'd calmed down from that, he said, "Hut one, hut two" under his breath, and we both started laughing all over again.

You know the strangest thing about that meal, though? The truckers at the other tables kept looking at me. Even when we weren't laughing. Kind of checking me out. No one had ever done that before. That was weird. It wasn't something I was used to.

Although right now as I'm sitting here writing, it occurs to me that maybe it wasn't the haircut. I was just more aware of, you know, looking okay. Maybe—probably not, and even writing this down makes me blush and feel like I'm being some sort of showoff, which I sure don't want to be—but maybe guys always looked at me and I just never even noticed.

23

Mom

10:18. I sort of glanced at the alarm clock and then sat bolt upright because I was supposed to be up five hours ago! The milking! I pushed back my hair and had another heart attack because my hair was gone. My fingers were going along and then they fell off a cliff because there wasn't any more hair there. Then—whoosh—everything came back: the banquet, the haircut, the drive back from Madison and Curtis's talk about dentists, the truck stop, our arrival home at four a.m., both of us crawling into bed—

I fell back, a little stunned. Curtis wanted to be a dentist? I mean, Amber was one thing, but this was totally out there. I lay there thinking it over. It was funny. It was downright hilarious, when you think about it. Curtis, of all people . . .

You know how on TV sometimes they have that bit about the good angel and the bad angel? Well, right then and there my good angel, which I didn't even know I had, said to me that if I ever made fun of what he told me I would go straight to hell. Which is true. And I just want you to know I will never do it. So I guess that good angel did her job.

As I lay there thinking about all this, there was this little squeak in the hall and a knock on the door and Mom said, "Dorrie, are you awake?" It occurred to me later that she might have been pacing outside my room for hours, and that squeaky floorboard might have been what woke me up in the first place. But I didn't think of that at the time.

"Can I come in?"

"Okay," I said, even though I wasn't much in the mood for company.

So she came in and settled on the edge of the bed. "How'd you sleep?" she asked, looking at me. Only she didn't look at me because if she had she would have noticed that most of my hair was gone and I looked totally different. She wasn't looking at me at all. She was in some completely different place.

"Okay," I said. But I had the feeling that I could have said, Not a wink, and she wouldn't have noticed.

She sat there for a while rubbing my knee through the covers, not saying much.

Finally, I asked, "Is everything okay?" Because I was beginning to wonder who died. Maybe she had some news from Win or Bill she needed to share.

"Oh, it's fine," she said, looking out the window like she'd never seen it before.

So I started looking out the window too, just for something to do, at the frilly curtains from when I was eleven and

Mom decided it was time to redo my room. "You're not a little girl anymore, you're almost a teenager," she'd said, which was something I wanted to hear only slightly more than that I was about to get a lobotomy. And she'd put up this flowery wallpaper and white curtains, and fixed up Grandma Joyce's sewing table for my desk, and a couple other things that, well, they weren't me then and that aren't me now. I stared at those curtains, thinking that maybe I could slip them under the bed. Just have shades like the boys do.

"I remember when you were born," Mom said, making me jump. "I was so happy to have a little girl." Then she didn't say anything else, letting that just hang in the air.

"Oh," I said.

"I didn't have a little girl for long." She smiled kind of sadly. "I don't think you know how proud we are of you. Your father, he's told me at least a dozen times in the past six months how proud he is." She looked at me again—looked at me without looking at me, if you know what I mean. "If it hadn't been for you, we would have had to sell the farm. Did you know that?"

I shook my head. This was getting heavy. The problem was, I didn't know where it was going. She was saying some amazing things, but I was so busy waiting for the But that I didn't have anything left to appreciate them. They were just wasted.

She sighed again, rubbing my leg like it was a magic lamp

or something. "I just want you to know that you don't have to prove anything to us. To me or Dad. We love you so much."

Again: what was coming next? Because you don't just say words like that just to put them out there. Not those words. Not in my family, anyway.

"You don't have to play football for us."

"What?" I asked, sitting about a foot higher in bed.

"Your trying out, it makes me see how we haven't been appreciating you enough. But you don't have to—"

"How do you know about that?"

Mom eyed me. "Jeff Peterson came to the Board of Ed meeting last night to give us a heads up."

"Oh," I said. "I didn't know about that."

"Neither did I," she said, probably sharper than she meant to.

Ouch. I mean, there you are, acting principal, and the football coach stands up and says your daughter wants to play football? Of course everyone would look at you, and you'd look pretty stupid when you said you had no idea. The last thing I wanted was to make her life any harder than it already was. Here she was, stuck between Dad and Win and Bill, with Curtis not talking, and it wasn't fair for her to go around thinking I was losing it too. I didn't mind Dad thinking that, but it wasn't fair to her.

Finally, just to say something, I blurted out, "It's got nothing to do with Dad." I tried to find the words. "It's just that I spent all summer feeling like I was doing everything I was supposed to, and seeing everyone around me doing what *they* were supposed to, and no one seemed happy. They just seemed caught. And I was so unhappy I tried to find something that made me happy, and then I had this idea of playing football. And that made me happy. So I thought I'd try."

Whew.

Mom swallowed. "Do you think I'm unhappy?"

Oh, boy. Out of the frying pan into the fire. "No," I lied.

"Because I really like my job."

"But it takes all your time," I said.

"Well, teaching and administration, that's a lot."

"But you're never home," I said.

Mom looked away. I had this feeling she was doing everything she could not to lose it. "It's just," she said, "that there's not a whole lot for me at home right now."

That hung there in the air for about a million years. What do you say to that? Maybe Oprah would know what to say. Maybe if we were driving back from Madison I could come up with something. But I didn't have two or three exits to work it through. I had only my crummy old bed, and that wasn't good enough.

"They offered me the job," she said, so quietly it took me a couple moments to register. "The principal job. Give up teaching and just do that."

"Wow." I chewed on that for a little bit.

"What do you think?" She asked it like my opinion really mattered to her.

I thought about her saying how much she liked her job. Just visiting her office, you could see how happy it made her. "Go for it."

She burst into this huge smile and threw her arms around me.

Finally, just to get her off me, I asked, "Are you okay with me playing football?"

She pulled back and studied my face. "Oh! When did you cut your hair?"

"In Madison." I tried not to blush—she was really looking me over. "I spent all the money on it. I'm sorry."

"It looks great," she said, turning my chin.

"It didn't fit under the helmet," I said. "With the ponytail."

She brushed a wisp out of my face. "Oh, D.J."

"Did you tell Dad?" I asked. "About football?"

"I wanted to talk to you first. You don't have to be so hard on him, you know. He never wanted to be a farmer. He gave up a lot for this place."

"Jeez." Which Mom doesn't like, but there wasn't anything else I could think of to say.

She patted my knee. "He's not that unhappy. He loves to cook."

There was another long silence, but it was okay. I could hear Dad downstairs, banging around.

"I should go," Mom said, patting my knee again. "This was real nice, us talking."

"It was," I said, feeling like someone at the end of an Oprah Winfrey show.

"Do you really like football?"

I nodded.

"Then that's a good reason to play."

"If I make the team," I added.

"You'll make the team."

"You always say that," I said.

"I always know," she said with a smile, and she left.

I lay there for a while longer, staring out the window. And you want to know what I thought about? That maybe I should leave those curtains up just a little bit longer because my mom wanted them so much. For me, her only daughter.

24

WELCOME TO SCHWENKSVILLE

I spent Friday, what was left of it anyway, waiting for Brian to show up so he could see my hair and get all surprised about me playing football, now that Jeff officially said I could play. But then after lunch the phone rang and Mom answered it and said, "D.J., it's for you," with this little smile that I had no idea what to do with, and it was Brian.

"Hey," I said.

"Hey." He sounded like there was something wrong.

All I could think about was his bloody nose, and I started blushing.

"Hey," Brian repeated. Something was definitely wrong. "Listen. My dad works with this guy who has this house on Lake Superior. It's really cool. It's got a pool, and—anyway, he just invited us up. For the weekend."

"Oh," I said.

"And I was wondering—I know we're working out this afternoon and all, but I was wondering if it would be okay if I went."

"It sounds pretty great," I said. Because that's what you say.

"Hey, want to come?"

Which was just so completely out of the question, so wild and so crazy and so darn sad, that I had to laugh. "Sure," I said.

"Really? That would be so cool!"

And I couldn't tell if he was kidding, although he must have been kidding because there's no way in a million years that I could leave the farm and the calves and the twice-a-day milking, and more important, there is no way that anything in the world I do, ever, is cool. Except maybe my haircut. Which now he wouldn't be able to see.

"I can't," I said. "we're haying tomorrow. But thanks for asking."

"Oh. Do you need my help?" he asked. But it was obvious he didn't mean it.

"Nah," I said, my heart breaking.

"Then I'll call you Sunday night when I get back. Okay?"

"Sure," I said, counting the days. And that's how we left it.

I went back and sat down like nothing had happened because in our family that's what you do. And when Dad made a crack about knowing Brian would quit, I didn't say a word.

Grandpa Warren told me once that there's a town in Pennsylvania named Schwenksville, which just about knocked me out. A whole town full of Schwenks? Then he explained a little more that it was just named after someone with our name, which still tickled me a lot. When I got older, though, and I'd be stuck on the farm working while every other kid in the world was out having fun, I began to think of our place as Schwenksville. This little spot that I'd be stuck in forever with only my family.

The next three days, I was in Schwenksville. Dad's hip had healed enough that he could drive the tractor without it falling out or anything, which meant he could mow and roll and bale all by himself which I guess I should view as a good thing. But we still had to bring the hay in, me and Curtis, while Dad drove the hay wagon around the field and told us what we were doing wrong, him complaining nonstop about the weather when he wasn't complaining about us. And me the whole time thinking that if this was a real family I'd be off with Brian at Lake Superior if he even meant his invitation, which he probably didn't but he knew he could ask because I'd have to work. I couldn't figure out which was worse to think about, him meaning it or him not.

It was nice, though, working with Curtis. Sometimes we'd catch each other's eye and grin a little, and that was okay.

Saturday night I thought a couple times about calling Amber, I was so bored and lonely. But I couldn't. I mean, what were we supposed to say to each other? We couldn't even talk about my haircut, seeing as it would really hurt her feelings that I drove all the way to Madison instead of using her. And that's not even bringing up the, you know, big stuff, the stuff we *really* couldn't talk about, like Brian. And her. Mom even said that she hadn't seen much of Amber lately— I think she was trying, you know, to egg me into getting out or something—but I just mumbled that she was busy and changed the subject.

Sunday it rained and Mom insisted on taking me out shopping for school clothes, which is not one of my top thousand favorite activities, but she said if I stayed in the house moping I'd drive her to drink. So we went to this mall and along with jeans and T-shirts and stuff, Mom ended up getting me a couple new sports bras and some training shorts and things.

And you know what the nicest thing was? She never said a word. She never said that I'd need those clothes for preseason. She never pointed out how my old sports bras were covered with paint and all worn out because I'd worn them every day, without a shirt a lot of the time. She never asked when I was going to tell Dad about football, although I could tell it was just about killing her, my not doing that. Most important, though, she never pulled an Oprah about Brian. Because if she had, I would have died. Seriously. I would have broken into a million little pieces and died.

But she didn't, for the same reason she never got involved in The Fight to begin with, or mentioned she was e-mailing

Win and Bill. Or made me talk to Dad directly about cleaning the barn, or took me on for walking out on Sunday dinner that one time. Because that's not her job, not in our family, anyway. Her job is to keep the peace, make sure everyone is doing okay, and not say too much about it. And you know, my mom might not be the most perfect mother in the whole world, but on that score, at least, at keeping quiet about awkward subjects, she's pretty great.

So once I stopped being scared that she was going to Ask Something and stopped worrying that maybe I should, which would have messed this whole thing up again, it got to where we could just talk. And she told me about how excited she was to be principal, and how she needed to take all these education classes because apparently teaching sixth grade for twenty years doesn't count, and she just seemed so happy. It was great, actually. It was like we weren't even family, it was more like we were friends

We talked for so long that I even forgot about Brian, until I got home and Brian didn't call. He had promised to call me when he got back from the weekend and he didn't. If I ever have kids, which of course would depend on me meeting someone and getting married and everything, all of which I have real doubts about, but if I do, the one thing I'm going to teach them is that if they ever promise to call someone, they better keep that promise. You can wreck the car or flunk

out of school or anything you want. But if you break a promise like that, you're no longer my child.

Then I started getting worried that maybe something had
happened, like he and his folks had a car accident or something coming back from Lake Superior. And it got later and
later and I finally just called him.

His cell phone rang about three times and then he answered. "Hey! I was just thinking about you!" I could hear all
this noise in the background, music and people shouting and
laughing.

"Hey," I said, so happy to hear him. "I just, um, wanted to
make sure you're okay."

"Who's that?" a girl asked in the background.

"I'm doing great," Brian said to me, ignoring her. "It's
been totally insane. Practice starts tomorrow and everyone's
a little crazy. I wanted to stop by this afternoon and see
you—"

"Who are you talking to?" the girl asked. She didn't sound
too pleased. At least Brian was ignoring her.

"How about tomorrow after practice? Are you going to be
around?"

"Um, I think so. It's just that—" I started to explain about
football.

I could hear more laughter in the background. "I've got to
go! I'll see you then, okay?"

"Have fun," I said, but it sounded like he was already.

✱ ✱ ✱

So I lay in bed that night going over our conversation in my mind, thinking about how happy Brian sounded to be talking to me. Like he said, things are crazy the day before preseason. At least he'd wanted to stop by. I was extra relieved now that Mom had taken me shopping, because if I'd known I would have gone insane waiting for him to show up.

That girl in the background asking who I was—you know what I really liked? That he seemed a lot more interested in me than he was in her. I don't know who she was and I don't want to know, but she wasn't making him happy the way I was. Maybe, it occurred to me, he and I would end up as friends. I knew a couple people like that, guys with friends who are, you know, girls. Not girly girls or anything but just girls, which pretty much defines me to a T. I liked that idea. He'd come by tomorrow after practice, and if I made the team or at least made it through practice we'd joke about it, and maybe throw a couple passes or something, and try to figure out how to survive the season as enemies and everything. It was too bad, actually, that we were on opposing teams, because it would be awesome to play running back to his quarterback. Dominate offense and all. If I made the team, that is. If I made it through the first day of practice.

25

PRACTICE BEGINS

 $\mathcal{M}$ onday morning, after about the worst night of sleep ever, and after milking because who else was going to do it, I drove the pickup down to the high school. I really should have asked Dad if I could use it, but I sure didn't want to talk to him so instead I just took it.

I got there early and sat in the truck trying not to think too much because when I did all I could think about was all those guys looking at me when they figured out what I was doing. All those sullen, angry eyes.

Other kids arrived, a couple freshmen with their moms, who were going to stay on those hot bleachers for hours watching practice because I guess they didn't have anything better to do, and some other kids like Justin Hunsberger, whose eye I blackened back in fourth grade and who now played lineman, and who'd be about as happy to see me as he would a large stinking pile of dog poop. And if you're wondering, I feel the same way about him.

Just then there was a huge BANG and I jumped about four

feet in the air, and Kari Jorgensen jumped up next to my window, laughing hysterically because she'd snuck up on me and kicked the truck.

"You're here!" she said, like it was Christmas or something. "You're doing it!"

"Yeah," I said, trying to look like she hadn't just scared the pants off me.

"I was all worried you weren't going to be here because I'm not doing it without you. Hey, she's here!" she called to her brother.

Kyle studied me. "You're really going out for football?"

"I had to tell him," Kari explained. "He wouldn't believe me doing cheerleading."

Looking at Kari, though, it was hard to believe she ever did anything else. She was always really keyed up during basketball, but right now, all tan from the summer with her hair in this big ponytail and her shorts and everything, she looked great. She also looked like she'd had about eleven cups of coffee. I guess she was a little excited.

"Yeah," I said, "I'm going to try."

So because I couldn't put if off any longer, I got my duffel and my water bottles and everything and headed to the field. And let me tell you, it sure was nice walking with Kyle instead of by myself, and Kari jumping along next to us, telling us how cool we were.

"Nice haircut," Kyle offered. Which was nice of him.

Being captain and all, Kyle started stretching, and I stayed off to the side stretching too, glad to be doing something beyond stewing, and Kari found the cheerleaders and I guess she filled them in because a couple minutes later right across the field came this huge cheer: "Let's go, D.J., let's go!" So that the three or four guys who hadn't seen me before now did.

Right at that minute Jeff Peterson showed up and told everyone to run a couple laps.

Every time I passed the cheerleaders Kari would start up again, which was about the most embarrassing thing I've ever had happen to me in my life, in public, anyway, and it didn't help that Jeff gave me a look like it was my fault she was doing it.

So we all got back to the middle of the field and Kyle led everyone in warm-ups, and I was pleased to see how many guys could barely manage even fifteen pushups, because I guess when you're flipping burgers or shelving groceries you can waste the whole summer not training if that's the kind of person you are. And for once I was glad I was the other kind of person, the Schwenk kind who trained. Because I could tell it was really bugging a lot of guys how well I was keeping up, how I was keeping up better than some of them.

Then they got a lot madder during sprints, because on the first one I came in eighth, but by the tenth one I was fourth because, well, that's what I'd done all summer. One kid even threw up, which I thought was a little early considering we had all day of practice yet.

All this time no one said a word to me. A couple times guys would say things under their breath to each other; I couldn't hear what they were saying, but I figured they were talking about me. For all I know they could have been talking about socks. But I do know that no one was saying anything under his breath to me.

Some of the freshmen looked a little scared, to tell you the truth.

Then Jeff split up everyone by position and I headed on over to join the running backs and receivers. When I got there, Beaner Halstaad was sprawled out on the grass, grinning at me. "What the heck are you doing, woman?"

I shrugged. "Didn't have anything else to do this morning."

He laughed. I like Beaner, as much as I like Kyle. He's in my class, and the fastest kid in Red Bend. He's called Beaner because even when he was a baby he was as skinny as a beanpole. I run track with him and, well, he's fast. He's a receiver.

"They going to let you play?" he asked.

"Dunno. I've got to make the team first."

Then we started drills, Kyle and the other QBs passing while we took turns receiving. I was about fifth in line so I got a real chance to study Kyle's arm. It's not like I hadn't spent an awful lot of time watching him play, and when I came up he kind of gave me a look and went long, and I ran

for it and got it and you could tell, just from the way everyone turned away and went to the next play, that I'd done
okay.

And we did that for a while, me catching the ball every
time, just loving that feeling so much, and then we went to
running plays, and then Jeff had me cover Beaner during
some passing drills, which wasn't what I was expecting but it
was fun too because I'd had so much practice over the summer with Brian.

I'd hoped I'd be good at football, and it was turning out,
compared to a lot of boys in Red Bend, anyway, that I was.

For lunch I went out with Beaner and Kari and Kyle, although we were all too beat and hot to eat much. When we
got back, Jeff took us all into the gym, which was so nice and
dark and cool that it might as well have been heaven, and he
gave us each paper and a pencil and spread us out on the basketball bleachers to write our names and all.

"Well," he said finally, "I guess you all know D.J. Schwenk
is trying out for the team."

Everyone looked at me. Which was just superduper, I can
tell you.

"I'm not going to force this team to do anything they don't
want to do," Jeff continued, picking some mustache hair off
his tongue. "We've got a tough season ahead of us. Real
tough, and something like this, it could be real divisive if you

want to make it that way. It could bring down the team." He paused right there and looked up at me.

"D.J.?" he asked. "You got anything you want to say?"

Everyone stared at me twice as hard. If this was a movie or something I'd give this awesome speech and everyone would cheer and it would be great. But it wasn't a movie — it was my life. And I don't have much to say even in the best of situations.

Everyone waited.

"I guess —" My voice cracked. "If a guy wanted to go out for girls' basketball, I'd pretty much want to kill him."

A couple guys laughed like what I'd said was stupid.

But Jeff didn't look like what I'd said was stupid. He looked a little pleased, if you want to know the truth. "So I want you all to write the answer to this question: should D.J. Schwenk play on the Red Bend football team?"

Everyone stopped staring at me long enough to write. And I was supposed to write too! Jeez. Jeff should have warned me before putting me through the wringer like this.

Jeff stroked down his mustache. "Now I want you all to answer this: why?"

Underneath "Yes" I wrote, "Because she knows the game and has a good attitude." I thought "she" instead of "I" made it more official. Then I wanted to change it, and I guess some guys wanted to change what they said too because I could hear scribbling sounds everywhere, and I wondered if Jeff chose pencils without erasers on purpose. But I still liked that business about good attitude. That counts a lot. Ask my brothers. And I do have a good attitude if you forget about me wanting to kill any boy who plays girls' basketball.

So Jeff and his assistant gathered up all our papers and we all went back outside while Justin Hunsberger complained to everyone about how stupid that was, and then we scrimmaged. After a while Jeff told me to play defense and I ended up racing a lot against Beaner, who of course is super fast and who I could almost never catch, but when I did I always brought him down because, well, I know a lot about tackling and because he weighs pretty much nothing. Once Justin Hunsberger tackled me even though he was playing defense too, and Kyle called him a name and it got kind of ugly for a minute. Then, finally, we were done.

I walked out to the parking lot with Kyle and Beaner and a couple other guys, and Beaner was just going on and on about what a great linebacker I would be.

"I don't think so," I said. I didn't want to be a linebacker. I wanted to catch the ball like a baby. That's what I'd trained for.

"Oh, come on. You're better than Bill!"

Which made us all laugh because it so clearly was not true.

"You should do it," he said. "You're one heck of a tackler."

"I like running back." I grinned, so happy to hear this. "I like playing offense."

"Uh-oh," Kyle murmured.

I heard this really snotty voice say, "So how was practice, girls?" And standing right there in the middle of our parking lot were a bunch of guys in Hawley jackets. I'd forgotten about this part of preseason.

"Screw you," Kyle said like he was telling them to grow up.

"Jesus Christ," the Hawley guy said, "that's a girl! You've got a girl on your team!" The Hawley guys started cracking up.

"This isn't just a girl." Beaner stepped in front of me. "This is Bill Schwenk's sister. So you tell your wimp of a QB that he better watch his back because she is going to take him down." Which was about the bravest thing I'd ever seen, because Beaner is about half the size of those guys. He sure sounded tough, though.

By this time the Hawley guys were roaring with laughter. "You hear that, Nelson?" the first Hawley guy asked. "You're playing against a girl." And just then this guy who'd been talking to someone turned around, and I was looking right at Brian.

"Yeah," said Beaner. "She's playing linebacker."

Brian stared right into my face. I stopped breathing.

Beaner threw his bony arm around my shoulder. "She's been training all summer too. So you better start saying your prayers." And with his arm around my shoulders he walked me to the pickup. Which was good because my legs weren't working too good.

The look on Brian's face—I'll never forget it. It's carved into my brain forever. He looked like he'd been slapped. Like I'd slapped him.

When I got home it was almost milking time. Dad was at the kitchen window, and just from the way he was standing I could tell he was angry. Probably he was going to light into me about taking the pickup. So instead I went right into the barn in my stinky football clothes and everything to start milking.

I was halfway finished when Dad came in, using the cane just a bit because his hip was doing so well now. I was setting up Don Voss, a Wisconsin All-American back in the fifties who blew out his knee before he could go pro. Dad stood there for a minute and watched me in that way that always gets me nervous so I screw up even though I've done it a million times.

"I got a call just now from Randy Jorgensen," he said. Randy is Kari and Kyle's dad. "He told me you're going out for football."

Oh, I'd been dreading this moment. I didn't say anything, my head pressed against Don, feeling her warmth through my cheek. I couldn't even look at Dad.

"So are you?" he asked.

I nodded. I didn't know what to say.

There was this long silence. I could feel my heart beating,

waiting for Dad to make fun of me, bring up all the reasons I couldn't do it. Tell me what a mistake it was.

But it was even worse than I'd ever imagined. Instead he just poked at the manure gutter. "When's the last time you cleaned this out?"

"Yesterday."

"You better get on it, then. It's getting pretty ripe." And he walked out, not even really using his cane. Not bothering to even try to talk to me.

I stayed frozen there against Don Voss. I couldn't begin to tell you what I was thinking, my brain was so completely scrambled. I'll tell you one thing, though. A lot of things happened to me this summer. Really bad things, some of them. But that bit with Dad, well, that's what got to me the most. It just destroyed me.

I rested my head against Don Voss's soft flank and I sobbed like a little tiny baby.

26

Dog Days

Dad stopped speaking to me. You know about The Fight, how Dad hasn't talked to Win and Bill since Christmas? Well, now I was in their club. Yippee. On the other hand, I wouldn't have had much to say if Dad did talk to me, because I was so mad at him that the thought of trying to engage in some heart-to-heart Oprah Winfrey conversation was about number 34,679 on my list of priorities. So I guess to be fair, I should say that it wasn't so much that Dad wasn't speaking to me as we weren't speaking to each other. Which wasn't as awful as it sounds, because I was barely home, and when I was home I was either writing in my room or asleep.

The good news, I guess, is that Dad's hip was getting so much better that he could milk in the afternoons at least. Not that he told me or anything. He just started one day before I got home so I could just go on inside and ignore him back.

Brian also stopped speaking to me. But just like Dad — even though before this I'd never thought of the two of them having much in common — he also never told me.

Monday night I tried his cell phone and just got a recording. I'm not too good at leaving messages, so I hung up fast before it got to the beep part. Tuesday morning I got the recording again, which was frustrating. I couldn't stop thinking about that slapped look he had when he saw me, and how bad Beaner must have sounded, saying I was playing linebacker and that I'd take him down. I wasn't going to do either one of those things, but it's hard to explain that into an answering machine.

Besides, you know, I missed just talking to him. I'd notice something like the trim on the barn windows and I'd remember when we painted that and what we'd talked about, and then I'd wish we just could get together to joke about how much preseason sucked and just shoot the breeze the way we used to.

Finally, because I was getting a little nervous and everything, because I just wanted to talk to him, Wednesday night I called his house.

"Hello?" a woman answered.

"Um, hello," I said, sounding like the brain surgeon I always do on the phone. "Is, um, Brian there?" Then I added, remembering my manners finally, "It's D.J. Schwenk."

"Oh. D.J.," said the woman in this voice that I couldn't figure out at all. "Just a minute." She was gone for a while—long enough for me to start feeling sick—and came back on and said, "I'm sorry, but it looks like he left."

"Oh. Can you, um, tell him I called?"

"I'll leave him a note. Goodbye."

It was so obvious that he was really home — she might as well have said that Brian told her to say he was gone. And then it hit me all of a sudden that Brian's cell phone has caller ID. He knew all the time it was me calling, or at least someone from the SCHWENK, WARREN household because the phone's still in Grandpa Warren's name because we never got around to changing it. And he was probably betting it wasn't Curtis.

That's when I figured out he wasn't talking to me.

Well, of course he didn't want to talk to me, because he was spending all his time around Hawley guys. You heard how sweet they were in the parking lot. Those guys are evil. Okay, that's a little strong. But they're not good. I'd bet a million dollars they were tearing me to bits, making all these cracks about me and ragging on Red Bend, and saying all sorts of nasty things that would make anyone bummed out if they listened enough. That plus the shock of seeing me Monday afternoon, well, no wonder Brian wasn't talking.

So I gave this a lot of thought, trying to figure out how to handle it in a real Oprah kind of way, and finally I decided to throw a brick through his window. Ha ha, just kidding. Although what I came up with wasn't that far off. If he wasn't going to talk to me on the phone and we probably weren't going to run into each other, not until the scrimmage, which probably wouldn't be too good a place for a heart-to-heart conversation, I decided to go by his house before practice when he'd be sure to be there.

Which, I just want you to know, was real brave of me, and shows how serious I was.

So Friday morning I left home extra early in our rusty old pickup, right after milking so I missed breakfast even, and headed over to Hawley. Brian's house was really new-looking, with new little trees around it and all, with a bunch of other houses in what used to be a field. I even remember when it was a field, which makes me sound like Grandpa Warren or something, but it's true.

I didn't even make it to his house, though, because just as I was pulling onto his street his Cherokee came the other way. I'll tell you one thing: he sure looked surprised to see me.

I stopped right there in the middle of the street and rolled down my window, and I guess because he didn't have a choice, Brian rolled down his window too.

"Hey," I said.

He glared at me.

"What are you so mad about?"

"Tell me you don't know," he said bitterly. "I spent every day with you all summer, and you never *told* me?"

"About football, you mean?"

"Duh! Of course about football!"

"I didn't think it . . . mattered." Which wasn't quite true. There's a lot I would say if I could have this conversation over again. About me feeling like a cow, about my feelings for him, maybe even about Amber if we talked long enough. But I couldn't say all that right there in the street. I don't think that fast, and certainly not when I'm getting yelled at. Which I was.

"Do you think I'd train like that, every day, with someone who'd be playing against me? Would you do that if you were me? I trusted you. But you—you just used me."

I didn't have one word to say.

Boy, did Brian look mad. Mad and hurt. "You Schwenks, you're messed up. You might be good at football but you really suck at life." He shook his head in disgust. "When you don't talk, you know, there's a lot of stuff that ends up not getting said."

Which, sitting here now writing it down, sounds pretty obvious and a little stupid, even. But hearing it then, boy, it just about killed me.

I headed back to Red Bend on autopilot or something. How would I feel if I'd spent all summer playing pickup with someone only to find out they'd been planning the whole time to play against me? After learning all my weaknesses, all my tricks? If that happened . . . I could see how Brian was mad. Because I'd pretty much want to throttle whoever that person was. Training someone, that's a commitment you make. And by deciding to play myself, I'd broken that. I like to think of myself as an honest person. If I had to list what I like about myself, I'd put "honest" right near the top. But not telling someone something—even though I'd always planned on telling him once I was sure it was happening and all—after a while not telling is about the same thing as lying. I'd lied to him.

I didn't like thinking that at all.

It wasn't until later that I remembered I'd never had a chance to say that I wasn't even going to be playing line-backer. So I'd never even be on the field at the same time as Brian. We'd never really be playing against each other. But by the time I thought of saying that, well, by then it was way too late.

So that was how absolutely wonderful my life was at this point, and the only thing that made it that much better was that I had to spend every free minute I had, until I passed out in bed because I was so exhausted, working on English. Every afternoon I'd eat everything in the fridge and take a shower until the hot water ran out, standing there wishing Amber and I were still friends because then she could give me one of her amazing back rubs, missing her in a way just as much as I missed Brian. Then I'd head into my room the way Smut walks into the vet's. Which if you're wondering means I was pretty darn reluctant. Even though Mom had brought a good computer home from school because ours is so old it could probably use Dad's walker.

The only reason I was even writing at all was because by now everyone in town, in the whole state it seemed, knew about me and football. And if they found out I couldn't play because I'd flunked English and hadn't finished my makeup work, that would be just about the worst. I'd pretty much have to leave the country. So if you're ever looking for motivation, there's one idea. Get everyone talking and you'll be sure to do whatever it is you need to do. Well, maybe it wouldn't work for you, but it sure worked in my case. I mean, I hope it does. It's not over yet.

And it turned out, if you want to know the truth, that writing wasn't half as hard as I thought it would be. Except for the fact that all I could do was think about Brian and want to die.

One evening as I sat there staring out at the sunset and feeling like a dried-up old cowpie, Curtis stopped by my room.

"Hey," I said, not turning around. I could see his reflection in the window.

"Hey." He stood there all hunkered down and uncomfortable. Finally he asked, like he was offering to fall on a grenade or something, "Are you okay?"

"No," I said, because I was too beat to lie.

"Do you, um, like Brian?" Which I have to give him a lot of credit for because it was probably the bravest thing he's ever done, asking that.

"Yeah." I thought about it. "Yeah, I like him a lot."

"Oh." He stood there a bit longer. "I'm sorry."

I turned around to look at him standing there looking as cut up as I felt. It just about killed me, seeing how much he cared. "Thanks," I said. I meant it too.

27

MAKING THE TEAM

So I guess I should tell you before you bite your fingernails off worrying that I did make the team. Which didn't surprise anyone too much except Justin Hunsberger, who told anyone who would listen how stupid Jeff was, and I was, and everyone was except him. Then after a couple days Jeff took Justin into his office and told him—I heard later—that Justin was the only starter who'd voted against me and that Justin needed to find either a new attitude or a new team and maybe he'd better sit out practice until he decided which one it was going to be. Which really made Justin's day, I can tell you.

Just so you know, it wasn't like all the other guys on the team were in love with me and thought that having a girl on their football team was the best idea they'd ever heard in their entire lives. It was more that Red Bend is so desperate they'll take pretty much anyone. They'd take Smut, or that cow Don Voss even, if either one of them could wear a uniform and show some sign of beating Hawley.

Still, it was nice to know that most of the guys didn't hate me outright.

Practice, though, was brutal. I had it a bit easier than some because I was in shape, from working with Brian plus all that weightlifting known as farming. But the guys had one up on me because they were used to all that gear. Boy, does that suck. And I say this as someone who really loves football. I was awful glad I'd done all those sprints by myself in the heifer field just to get used to it. Because a two-hour practice in full gear on that burning-hot field . . . jeez. Let me just say that when basketball season starts I'm going to fly like a bird down that court. My feet won't even touch the ground. Assuming, that is, I survive that long.

Plus I had the whole burden of being a Schwenk. Which in some ways is good because it pretty much got me on the team, being Win and Bill's sister. If Amber had tried out, someone without that last name, they'd have eaten her for lunch. Not without a fight, though, if it was Amber, anyway. But because I'm a Schwenk and Schwenks work so hard, that meant I had to be at every practice from beginning to end, giving my Schwenk all. Which meant, say, that when Jeff wanted the water break to end and everyone to line up for sprints, he'd say, "Line up for sprints," and no one would move. And then he'd say, "D.J.?" and I'd get up—just like a cow but don't you make that crack—and head over to the end line. And then everyone else would have to stand up too, because I'd started it and I was a girl and also going to beat them if they didn't haul their butts.

Sometimes Jeff wouldn't say anything—he'd just look at me. And sometimes he'd just wait. I bet in his mind he was saying, D.J. Is Responsible, and my Schwenk radar would pick it up right through all that sweat and moaning and groaning, and I'd head out to the field and start. And then on the second sprint I'd be the first one on the line again. And the third sprint. And the fourth . . . Anyway, you get the idea. Basically, I was a big old Schwenk Motivator getting the rest of the team in shape.

Besides Justin Hunsberger and Schwenk motivation and all that, there were other teeny little problems too, like the whole locker room thing. I always figured I'd just go in a closet or something to put my gear on. I'd spent all summer around Brian, after all, without him ever even noticing, it seemed like, and any guy who wanted a glimpse of me in a sports bra, well, that's a guy who needs to spend a lot more time online.

But apparently I'm the only person in Red Bend who feels this way, because people kept calling Mom about it, and coming by the school, and Jeff had to get keys to the girls' locker room so I could change in there. Only most of the time the cheerleaders were in there too, which would have been awful if it hadn't been for Kari, who was in cheerleader heaven, and they'd all watch me suit up, asking all sorts of questions, and then when I was dressed a couple cheerleaders would hurry to the boys' locker room to say I was ready and try to go in with me. Jeff finally took them aside and I couldn't hear what he said except the word Distraction came up a couple times, and after that they got better about it. A little, anyway.

And then I'd sit in the locker room with the guys, and some of them would be jerks about jockstraps and stuff but most of them wouldn't, and Jeff would go over plays and workouts, preparing us for our first big scrimmage, the annual scrimmage less than two weeks away, on the Friday night before Labor Day, against Hawley.

And then we'd go out and practice until I could barely stand up.

The problem was that Jeff was working me an awful lot as a linebacker. (I guess I should explain that on teams as small as ours a lot of guys play both defense and offense. Justin Hunsberger, for example, plays both sides of the line.) But I didn't want to be linebacker! I hadn't had the guts to call Brian yet because I couldn't figure out what to say, but I knew for sure that telling him he was right and we'd be playing against each other wouldn't be too good.

Finally after practice one day I stopped by Jeff's little office, where he was studying a play sheet and tugging on his mustache.

"Coach? You got a minute?"

He settled back in his chair. "You betcha. How's it going there?"

"Okay." I wondered if what I was about to say counted as

good attitude. I didn't think so. "Listen, I know everyone's psyched to have me as linebacker because of Bill and all."

"Because of you." Which was nice of him.

"Thanks. Thank you. But, well, I don't want it."

Poor Jeff. Between me and football he wouldn't have any mustache left come November. "This have anything to do with that business between you and your brothers?"

I shook my head, twice as miserable now knowing that Jeff knew about The Fight. "I just . . . don't want to play defense on Friday."

"What makes you think you're playing?" he asked matter-of-factly. Meaning, here I was telling him what to do after two weeks of practice when there are guys who've been on the team for years who don't get to play.

So in a way I was twice as embarrassed that I'd sounded so full of myself. But I was pleased too, because now I wouldn't have to play against Brian.

"How you coming with your schoolwork?" Jeff interrupted my train of thought.

"I'm getting it done."

"Good," he said, and he went back to work and I left.

It wasn't until later that I realized I'd been doing all that English class writing for nothing.

Speak of the devil, that afternoon Mrs. Stolze came by and sat in the living room with a pencil and everything, reading what I'd written so far. I was so nervous that I ended up in the barn helping Curtis get ready for milking just for something to do. We didn't talk too much, though I did tell him that Shannon Kleinhart—she's one of the cheerleaders—just got her wisdom teeth out. That perked him up.

In the end Mrs. Stolze said I'd done enough for the scrimmage at least. I didn't have the heart to tell her I wouldn't be playing, so I just promised I'd get the rest to her by the first day of school. And then she left with a couple of Dad's brownies, which he'd been baking to show off. That smell hung like a big cloud over the house. It might have been why she was so willing to let me play, that happy brownie smell. It might not have been my work at all.

What was I going to say to Brian? I could do the bad-news-and-good-news bit, the bad news being that I was playing linebacker and the good news that I wouldn't be playing at all. That would be funny if we were still friends and all, but these days I didn't think I'd hold his attention long enough to get the words out. He'd probably just tell me again that my family really sucked at life.

Which we did. Because here we were at dinner—seeing as it was dinnertime and all, and we were sitting together chewing on something made out of hamburger—and we hadn't said a single word.

So I said, just to shake everyone up, "Looks like I'll be playing linebacker."

Everyone stopped eating. I might as well have said that I

was going to run around buck naked. Isn't that just the saddest thing you've ever heard? I'd been playing football for almost two weeks and I couldn't even say that fact out loud in my very own house. Not because anyone told me not to, but just because, well, we hadn't talked about it. And once you don't talk about something in our family, then, well, you can't bring it up.

But I had.

Curtis slouched down even lower in his chair.

I just kept plowing along. "On the football team."

"That's great," Mom managed to get out. I'm sure she'd noticed by now that Dad and I weren't talking, but she sure hadn't said anything about it. Maybe she figured that eventually I'd move out and then she could just start e-mailing me.

So we all went back to eating, except that we were on code red family drama alert. Eventually we finished, and Curtis and I carried our plates to the sink because the last thing we needed was Mom getting hysterical.

All this time Dad hadn't said a word, just stared into space, working away at his hamburger thing. I paused in the doorway and looked at him, still feeling raw and angry about our whole messed-up family and everything we weren't.

"Are you going to tell me to clear out too?" I asked, because that's what Dad had said to Win and Bill during The Fight. And then I left. But he—well, there's a chance he started to say something but I was already out of the room, and there was no way in heck I was coming back. So I guess I'll never know for sure.

Instead I decided right then and there to make the call. So before I lost my nerve or anything, I stomped up to Mom and Dad's room and shut the door and dialed the phone.

He didn't pick up. I figured he wouldn't, what with his cell phone saying SCHWENK, WARREN and all. I listened to it ring and ring, and then the message started and it almost killed me to hear his voice, his deep voice that always sounds like he's saying something sexy because he's probably hoping it's a girl, a real girl and not me, calling: "I'm busy, leave a message." And then the beep.

I took a deep breath and said, "Hey, Bill, it's me, it's D.J. You know, your sister? I was just, you know, thinking about you and, you know, thought I'd call. And anyway, I hope you're okay and I hope preseason is going okay and all, and I don't know if Mom told you but I'm playing—well, never mind. It's nothing. Anyway, you know, so, have a good day and everything and, well . . . bye."

I hung up, and then sat there for about five hours, staring at the phone and wishing there was some way I could call back and erase my entire message, which—I'm not sure about this but I'm willing to guess—was the stupidest voice mail in the history of the world, going back to the Egyptians and everything.

But at least I'd called. I'd punched that bruise and I'd called my brother.

✳ ✳ ✳

In the morning I left before anyone else got up because I just couldn't handle one more minute of Schwenk family misery. And we had our practice and after that a scrimmage, offense against defense to practice for the Hawley game, with people in the stands watching us and everything so it felt almost like a real game only without that energy and anger. Sometimes I played linebacker on defense, and sometimes I played running back, usually halfback. I got to catch the ball some but most of the time we worked on running plays when Kyle would hand me the ball and I'd try to cross the line of scrimmage and move it downfield. Or I'd block for someone else like Kyle who was carrying. Let me tell you, blocking is hard work. It's like haying in that you're using your whole body, throwing all your weight into a thrusting jerk. Only hay bales don't fight back.

Plus there were a million things I didn't yet know about football, little tricks and habits and facts that you learn only from years and years of playing, that you can't pick up on the sidelines as someone's little sister. I had to focus like crazy just to feel like I was barely on top of things.

Then, right before the last play, Kyle elbowed me. "Isn't that your old man?"

Jeez, it was. And he'd been there a while too. Not that I'd noticed it was him—which I felt stupid about now that I did—but I'd known there was someone sitting in that spot. It wasn't like this was the first time in my life Dad ever watched me play. He and Mom come to every basketball game they can, especially the night ones after milking, and he came to track meets too if his schedule worked out. But still, this was different, and I knew it. And you know it too.

So we got in a huddle, me trying really hard not to think about Dad, what he thought of the team and my playing, what sort of smart-mouthed comments he'd make, and then the huddle broke and I had to ask Beaner what the play was. He whispered it back, and luckily it was a passing play so I didn't have to do much except keep from tripping, and Beaner caught it like the pro he is, and practice was over.

Well, it was over in the sense that we stopped working, but Jeff talked to us in the locker room for a while, reminding the players—which didn't include me—what time to show up tomorrow and the JV—including me—to show up to watch, and how important this scrimmage was and how many people would be there, like this was all stuff we weren't aware of. And then we went back outside, with the stands a lot emptier than they'd been earlier, although Dad was still there, I could see. I cleaned up as slowly as I possibly could because the very last person I wanted to talk to was him. Jeez, I was supposed to listen to his cracks? Or his silence, which was even worse because then I'd just imagine what he was thinking, and I have a pretty active imagination. Maybe when he started I'd just say in a real Oprah voice that I had to focus on the scrimmage and I didn't want to hear any criticism. Only I wasn't sure I had the guts to do that—

"Hey there, Mr. Schwenk," Kyle said. "How'd we look?"

Holy cow, Dad was right behind me. I didn't turn around.

"You got an arm there, son. Like someone I know," Dad said.

"It's not much," said Kyle, bursting with pride. "What'd you think of D.J.?"

I froze right there on one knee, cleats in my hand. I could hear Jeff fifteen feet away, rustling papers on his clipboard. I could hear cheerleaders working in the next field. I could hear a small plane in the distance. I could hear the grass growing, it felt like.

"She looks okay," said Dad slowly. "She really does. It's something to be proud of."

"You hear that, D.J.?" Kyle slapped me on the back. "Your dad's proud of you."

"You ready, Dad?" I asked, gathering up my duffel bag. Because I wasn't going to make a big deal out of it in case you're wondering. But it, well, it wasn't the worst thing he could have said.

We set off back across the field together, Dad and me, taking our time on account of his hip. "I checked on the heifers this morning," he said, looking off into the distance.

Well, that just about gave me a coronary. Because of course right there in the middle of the heifers is our football field all marked out in lime, with little flappy car dealer flags around it and everything.

"Oh," I said, adjusting my bag.

"That's quite a setup you got. You do that all by yourself?"

I shrugged. "Yeah. With, you know, Brian. We did some training up there."

"So that's what you two were up to all summer." He sounded amused, frankly.

I tried not to blush. "What'd you think of the scrimmage?"

"You looked good." He looked around at the bleachers, the peeling Red Bend Wolves sign. "It takes me back. Makes me wish I'd stayed in coaching."

"Well, why don't you? They always need an assistant."

He waved this away. "The only thing I'm halfway good at is farming."

"You can cook," I offered, without even having to really think about it.

Dad eyed me. "You don't even like my cooking."

"I do too. It's good. It's real good."

"You never said anything."

"Well, I didn't want it to go to your head."

Dad laughed and messed up my hair. "It looks okay, that haircut," he said.

"Makes me look like a boy," I grinned.

"No, it doesn't. It doesn't at all," he said, settling his arm around me.

And that's how we walked off the field, the two of us together, Dad's arm around my shoulders.

28

THE SCRIMMAGE

$\mathcal{I}$ spent Friday so relieved that I wasn't playing, especially when I went down to Jorgensen's Ice Cream and watched Kyle wandering around looking green and Kari working herself up into a tizzy for her very first game. Cheerleaders are a lot braver than people give them credit for, people like Amber and me anyway. But then just as I got home Jeff Peterson called and told me to suit up.

"I'm playing?" I gulped in a not very Schwenk way.

"You're going out with the team" was all he said.

I couldn't figure out what he was talking about until I got to the locker room that afternoon and found the guys in a lather, even Kyle who's usually puking by now.

Beaner frowned at me. "Did Hawley's QB work for you guys?"

How the heck did he find *that* out? "Brian Nelson? Uh, yeah, a little."

Kyle snorted. "Did he sue you?"

"What?" I asked.

"Because he's suing the school," Beaner scoffed.

"What? Why?"

Beaner grinned at me, amused as all get-out. "Because of you. Claims you're ineligible."

And of course at that very moment Jeff stood up to give his little pep speech, and I was left there with my mouth hanging open, trying to figure out what was going on. Brian was suing Red Bend? It must be his dad, Mr. You're-Always-Perfect Nelson, who probably knew from Brian about my grade issues, or at least about me being a girl. But still, suing us . . . jeez. I felt sick just thinking about it.

I didn't hear much of Jeff Peterson's speech, but what I heard sounded good. I mean, how many different speeches can there be? I've heard a bunch before every basketball game, and little ones at every b-ball time-out. But he did a good job. Said that he'd be a lot prouder of us if we lost as a team than if we won as showboaters, which isn't true but it was still good to hear. He kind of looked at Justin Hunsberger when he said that showboating line, in case the point wasn't clear enough.

Then we had to line up and go out on the field, the bleachers full and people standing all around the track outside the fence to watch, and we went out one by one while the announcer said our names, and that's when I figured out why Jeff wanted me there, because when my name was announced there was extra cheering from the Red Bend side and a bunch of booing from the Hawley side, and I guess Jeff decided I needed to be out there rubbing Hawley's nose in it. Our announcer is a Red Bend mortician who's been doing it for years. The joke is that he's the kiss of death for our team, but he sure loves his job and he buys a big ad on the back of the program every week and everything. He couldn't help but point out that I was Win and Bill Schwenk's sister just in case, you know, there was someone in the crowd from Iceland or someplace who wasn't aware of the connection.

If nothing else, I was glad Dad already knew I was playing because it sure would have been a shock if he'd found out then.

Kyle won the coin toss and opted to receive the kickoff, and the game began. It was kind of weird, actually, because I've always been a starter on basketball and I play every game until I foul out, so watching the game from the sidelines without feeling angry or guilty about all those fouls, that was new for me. And it would have been fun too, except that I was watching my team lose.

We were holding it together pretty well, all things considered. Red Bend made it all the way to the 23-yard line before Hawley shut us down, then we lost on downs and Hawley got control. When the sides switched — our defense going in against their offense — Brian went as QB, I noticed.

I watched the game as closely as I've ever watched football in my life, especially because I knew a whole bunch more after playing for two weeks. Hawley's top receiver didn't have Beaner's speed—he plays baseball in the spring for Pete's sake, and no one ever built speed doing that—but he could get where he needed to go, and Brian was looking really good. Even the announcer pointed it out. Finally Hawley scored, on a scrabbling little running play from the 15, and then made their extra point so the score was 0–7.

I could go through the whole game play by play, but I'll spare you except to say that for most of the half Hawley's offense was on field with Brian playing the game of his life. Red Bend held them off as well as we could, but then with about eighteen seconds left, they scored again with a field goal, so the score was now 0–10.

Then the buzzer sounded and the half was over.

And then as everyone was walking off the field, a Hawley player—I don't know his name and I didn't even notice his number, which is too bad because in a weird way I'd like to thank him—he came up behind me and gave my butt a squeeze and said "dyke" under his breath. Just like that.

Now. Let me say first of all that I am not completely unfamiliar with trash talk. For one thing I play basketball with Amber Schneider, who can make a point when she wants to. And I know how rough it can get on the football field. From the stories Bill tells, I'm surprised fights don't break out all the time. And I know all about getting patted on the butt. Heck, if Dad squeezed Mom like that she'd act like he'd given her flowers. You watch pro ball and those guys spend so much time with their hands on each other's rear ends, you'd think they were feeling for diamonds or something. If a Red Bend guy did that to me I wouldn't think twice about it.

But it wasn't Red Bend. It was a guy from Hawley. And he was doing it, and saying that word, simply to be a jerk. Pure and simple. To hurt my feelings. And I didn't like that one bit, especially given that we were down by 10 and hadn't even come close to scoring.

I stomped off the field just so furious. Because, you know, if there's one thing that got established over this summer, over this miserable, dog poop summer, it's that I'm not a dyke. Call me any other name you want, I'd probably deserve it, but I am definitely into guys. And it hit me all of sudden how Amber, my best friend Amber, was going to have to put up with that word her whole life. Jerks who'd call her names just because. I hadn't been the best of friends to her these past few weeks. I hadn't called her or reached out to her even though she's probably been hurting pretty bad, and normally I'd feel pretty guilty about that. I mean, I should. I acted pretty rotten to her. But all that guilt that I should have been feeling went right into rage at Hawley instead.

And then at that moment I saw Brian with his arm around a Hawley cheerleader, a little blond girl with skinny little legs, heading to their locker room, and all of a sudden something inside me just plain old snapped. That plus the nasty name I'd just been called that wasn't even true because of Brian . . .

And I started thinking.

Brian, you may have noticed, was Hawley's starting quarterback. Did you notice that? He *started*. He wouldn't be starting without me. He wouldn't be starting—and playing so well that even our mortician noticed—unless Jimmy Ott had sent him to our farm and insisted I train him. And what thanks did I get for that? A lawsuit, that's what. When I'd spent every day all summer coaxing this spoiled rich kid off his butt as he'd roll in at whatever time he pleased in his brand-new Cherokee, handling him like he was brain-damaged or something through every weight workout, every drill, every sprint, every pass he missed so he'd get it right next time. All for free. When we actually could use the money a lot. For nothing except one stinking little thank-you he offered up once like it was a gold ring or something. Just so he could be starter. And now he wouldn't even look me in the eye.

So I hadn't told him about football—so what. Well, not quite. There were some times over the summer when it might have been, you know, appropriate for me to mention it. Sort of pauses in the conversation when I could have brought it up without too much trouble. And I sure didn't mean for him to find out about it standing there in the middle of Red Bend parking lot with his scummy Hawley friends. I'd meant to tell him on that day he went on vacation instead—the day he *quit*—and then I figured I'd tell him when he came by the farm after the first day of practice. If he'd told me on Sunday night he'd be going to Red Bend High School, I would have warned him. But he didn't tell me on Sunday night because he was too busy partying. Maybe if he'd spent just a couple more seconds on the phone with his training partner—his official summer trainer, appointed by Jimmy Ott himself—he'd have learned something. But no, he had to get back to his party and his stupid friends and all those girls.

And wait a minute. Who were those girls, anyway? Who was that girl who kept pestering Brian when he was on the phone with me? Here he was all mad at me for not telling him stuff, and what was he doing? Was he telling me about the girls in his life? No. He mentioned his breakup but did he say one word more? No. So I couldn't ask about it—my mother wasn't Oprah Winfrey. He bragged so much about his family . . . Well, I'm sorry, but if you're going to go around talking about your feelings, the least you could do is tell a girl about the other girls in your life. Especially if you're going to *kiss* that girl, that first girl who doesn't know.

Unless, that is, you're the kind of guy who goes around doing that. You know the type? The guys who go around hitting on girls when they don't mean it? You know who does that? Jerks. That's who.

Which makes his asking me to go to Lake Superior with him that much worse. Because we both knew I couldn't go. It was like he was throwing me a bone or something. Like a dad who tells his kid they'll get a pony after they move when they're never going to move. That's what it was. He was just playing with me. I was the dumb farmer who'd spent the summer training him—though I'm sure he gave *himself* all the credit for that—and now he was back with a pretty girlfriend and his scumbag Hawley friends, and he would never think about me for one second ever again as long as he lived. Except to sue me.

By this time we were all sitting in the boys' locker room, the guys slumped on benches, looking just whipped. But I wasn't whipped. I was furious. Boy oh boy, was I mad. Can you tell? It was like all the things that I should have been mad about for weeks and weeks just built up inside me until I ended up one huge volcano of angry D.J.

Jeff was talking but I didn't even hear it because I was too busy getting madder and madder at Brian. And at myself too, for putting up with it, for not seeing it. Remember how upset I was when I figured out I was a cow? This was twice as bad. I'd taken so much from Brian, his little jokes and the little family secrets he'd confess, the way he'd brush against me sometimes, the way he'd work without his shirt on, me mooning over him like a stupid heifer, when he was just using me and I was too dumb to see. Well, I saw it now.

Then I noticed guys looking at me kind of funny, and I finally focused on Jeff. "You're playing like a bunch of girls out there!" he barked. "Like little girls! What do you have to say to that?"

There was this long, ugly silence.

"Ask her what she thinks about playing like a girl," Justin Hunsberger sneered.

Everyone turned their sweaty heads in my direction.

"Let's take them apart," I said, my voice kind of loud in that silent room.

A couple guys blinked.

"Let's go out there and destroy them. Let's leave them for dead," I said, my voice shaking, I was so keyed up.

"Yeah!" said Beaner. "Let's do it!" A couple other guys sat up a bit.

Jeff studied me sitting there so mad I was trembling almost. "You remember Bill's game?" He was asking everyone, but I felt like he was talking just to me.

Kyle sat up a bit more. "That's my ball," he whispered.

"I'm gonna get that ball," Beaner growled under his breath.

You could see other guys, the guys who'd been freshmen and sophomores when Bill was playing, starting to perk up.

"What did he say?" Jeff asked the room.

"That's my ball!" several guys called back.

"I'm gonna get that ball!" Beaner snarled.

"We're the Red Wolves!" shouted Kyle, acting—finally—like a captain. "What do wolves say?"

Everyone growled, getting into it. Me too. It felt great, actually, putting all my fury into that mean and ugly noise.

"What do wolves say!" he barked, getting into it now.

We all roared back to him.

"I can't hear you!" he shouted.

We roared until the room shook.

"You remember Bill! Come on! Let's hear it!"

We screamed, we pounded on the lockers. Beaner howled to the moon.

"Let's hear it! Again! Again! Again!"

We yelled and screeched and banged until Jeff Peterson waved for silence. He reached his hand out. Twenty-eight hands slapped down on top of his. Kyle threw open the door and raced onto the field, the team behind him. I came last, on purpose, next to Jeff. As we trotted out I said to him, real softly, "I need to play."

29

THAT'S MY BALL

Jeff put me in too. Maybe he was desperate. Or maybe, I don't know, maybe he could just tell. Because when we took the field for Beaner's kickoff I was so mad at Hawley and Brian, so mad at myself for being such a moron all summer, that I was ready to just destroy whoever got in my way. The Hawley players lined up at the other end, Beaner gave this nice long kick, and I charged down the field ready to tear to pieces whoever came my way carrying that football.

Only someone else got to him first, tackled him at their 40, and the second half of the game really began.

We, Red Bend defense, came out of our huddle and watched the Hawley players get in position. Brian lined up behind his center, waiting for the snap, and just for a moment our eyes met. He glared at me and I glared right back, thinking to myself that if he wanted to screw me over, I'd screw him right back. I'd plow right through that line and I'd—

Then he looked away and his face changed just a little bit, and I had this little pang. After all, he'd been my friend for a while, my closest friend, and by playing linebacker against him, I was about to destroy that friendship forever. And it hit me right in the gut what I was doing.

And then I scored.

I know Brian Nelson is never going to read this, and even if he did read it I know he wouldn't believe me. But I just want to say now, even though it sounds really pathetic, that I didn't want to. I mean, I didn't mean to. Listening to him call the play I wasn't thinking to myself, Here I am playing my very first football game and what I want to do more than anything is score against the guy I'm in love with who I spent all summer training. That's not what I thought. Really. But then he took the snap and I could see by where he was moving and looking and how the receivers ran that it was going to be a passing play to his left. And when he threw that ball I knew, just from having watched him throw a football three thousand times, where it was going to go. And without even thinking about it—maybe because I spent all summer running after his passes, or maybe because in football that's just what you do—I took off. That Hawley receiver, he was heading for where the ball was supposed to go but instead I was heading for where the ball was actually going. Which was only a difference of about two feet but sometimes two feet can count for a lot. And just as that receiver was reaching I reached up too, and I grabbed it out of the sky and tucked it under my arm just like a little baby, and without even thinking really I spun and took off for our goal line.

Did you ever have a dream where everything goes wrong? Where no matter what you do nothing works? Or not even a dream, but just a day where that happens? For me right at that instant it was just the opposite. I started running and all of sudden there was nothing in front of me but green grass. Like I was running in the heifer field. A couple Hawley players went for me but I got ahead of them, and then this other Hawley player—their fullback, I think—came charging at me and out of nowhere came a blur of Red Bend uniform blocking for me, and then there was nothing ahead of me, nothing except the 40-yard line, the 30, the 20, the 10, and then the goal line, me running like I could run forever with that baby of a ball in the crook of my arm.

And I crossed the goal line and banked a turn and tried to catch my breath, and all of sudden the noise hit me like a wall, everyone screaming like the world had stopped. Which, thinking about it now, I guess for a second or two it did.

The Red Bend players piled on top of me and pounded on me and smacked me so much it felt like I was being mauled, and what could I do but be thrilled to pieces and say how it was really nothing. Then Beaner, who's also our place kicker, which I forgot to tell you before, made the extra point, and all of a sudden the score went from 0–10 to 7–10, which is a lot better-looking if you ask me.

And then jogging back to our bench, a group of guys slapping me on the back and the crowd still screaming away, I looked up in the stands and there, sitting next to Mom and

Dad and yelling his lungs out, was my brother Bill. And right next to him was this huge black guy who had to be his roommate Aaron Johnson.

Well. Scoring a touchdown on an interception against your archrival, that's a feeling you don't get to feel too often, and it's pretty special, I'll have you know. But scoring a touchdown on an interception against your archrival while your Division 1 football–playing brother who hasn't talked to you in months is watching . . . I don't think there are words for that. I don't think there are words to describe everything going through my brain and my heart. The best I can come up with is this:

I was filled with joy.

And that joy poured into my blood, into my bones, and it mixed with my rage at Brian and my disgust with Hawley, and I think it even caught a little of Win's intensity and Bill's craziness, which makes sense seeing as we share a gene pool and all, and I went back on the field for the kickoff to Hawley, and I was possessed.

And with the kickoff Hawley ended up around the 35-yard line this time, and we lined up to meet them, listening to Brian screaming at everyone on his team not to screw up. He hadn't screamed at them in the first half, but he sure was now. Just like he used to. I felt a little bad about it. I really did. I felt bad that I'd taken advantage of my knowledge of his playing ability. But that little guilty feeling was pretty much overwhelmed by my disgust at how he was yelling at his teammates when he should have been pumping them up, plus my utter disgust at the fact that he was suing the school. And so I muttered under my breath, "Where's your father now, Brian?"

The bad news is that Justin Hunsberger happened to be standing near me when I said this, and he heard it. I found out later that when I'd been making that long run downfield for the touchdown and that Hawley fullback was going for me, it was Justin who'd blocked him. Which was really big of him when you think about how much we hate each other. But anyway, Justin heard me and right away he picked it up: "Where's your daddy, Nelson? Where's your daddy?"

And the other guys on my team started trash-talking too: "Who you going to sue, Nelson?" "Did your daddy tell you to say that?" And so forth. Well, this didn't sit too well with Brian, and I felt bad about starting it even though I didn't mean to and also, I was thinking at the moment, he kind of deserved it. Anyway, everyone lined up and Brian called a play but right after the snap Justin Hunsberger broke through the line and sacked him.

"Oooh," I could hear Justin sneer. "Does little Bwian have a little boo-boo? Does he want his daddy to kiss it and make it better?"

Brian didn't say anything but he looked at me like he wanted to kill me. And it really cut me. Because I know what it's like to take garbage from Justin Hunsberger, and of all the people I'd want knowing about Brian's family, Justin would be very last on the list.

But then I heard out of the stands, over all that screaming and cheering, "That's my ball! That's my ball!" Bill was bellowing. And then Aaron started chanting it too, and the guys on the field all around me picked it up, hollering it before each snap. For the record, I will say I never shouted it with them. But a couple times, a couple times during Brian's countdowns, right before the snap when I was bent down ready to burst out, I'd whisper it to myself. And then, full of Win's intensity and Bill's craziness, I'd explode.

So after those first couple plays, my touchdown and Justin's sack, the second half calmed down a little. Brian stopped passing because most of the time when he tried it me or someone else from Red Bend would be right there, and so that left Hawley with just running plays. And they'd churn their way through a couple downs until we'd stop them, and then we'd go in and manage a down, maybe three, until we got stopped, and that's how the game went. Only it was different from the first half because, well, because I wasn't the only one who was full of crazy intensity. We all were. Instead of it being a big strong school against a little weak school, it was kind of even. We knew it. Hawley knew it, or else why would Brian be bawling his team out every chance he got? And everyone in the stands knew it. And they were, well, they were pretty loud.

Whenever Hawley's offense left the field, I could see Brian shouting at Jimmy Ott. In case you're wondering, even though Jimmy's practically our uncle and he eats over all the time, it wasn't like he spent the whole game telling everyone to be nice to D.J. Schwenk. He got really mad at the ref for not calling me on interference once, and he was pretty vocal about telling Hawley to block me. But even so, Brian would go up to him and start screaming, basically, and Jimmy would scream right back.

And then Brian would have to go in with the whole Red Bend defense making fun of his dad, asking if he was going to sue them, asking if they were hurting his feelings. It got pretty rough, to tell you the truth. Sitting here now writing about it, I see that Hawley isn't the only football team in Wisconsin with jerks on it.

But Brian—I have to admit Brian kept playing. He didn't quit, and he even stopped yelling at his team. Instead he got quiet, which was a lot more intimidating. He'd come out of the huddle like a general or something—like Win does—and he'd bark out orders with no other talk, and those Hawley players would fall in line like soldiers.

But even so, we held them off. And then finally there we were seven yards from Hawley's goal line with only twenty-eight seconds left. Football games really end like this, not just in the movies. Only in real life we'd get slaughtered, Hawley would intercept us and win 7–17 instead of 7–10. That's what reality is in Red Bend, Wisconsin.

So there we were with two downs left, with me playing halfback because Joe Krazuk had messed up his ankle again, the left one he's got to be careful about because he broke it last winter playing ice hockey, and Jeff had put me in instead. Now. Let me say that at this point in the game I was so sore, just so destroyed, because football it turns out is a really brutal sport, that all I could think about was how I was going to have to play ten more games this season. And then I'd think about my brothers playing college ball against real opponents, real scary ones, and get even more impressed with them than I normally am. Because all I wanted was a long, *long* hot shower and a cool bed. And maybe a whole bottle of aspirin. And then the same thing again tomorrow.

So we got into the huddle and I guess maybe Kyle saw that I was whipped because he called for a trap using me as a lure but with Kyle really taking it himself. We lined up and everyone hunkered down like total pros all ready to block for me. And Kyle called it, and the center snapped it back and Kyle passed it to me. Only he didn't, he just faked it, and I did my very best with the three brain cells I had left to pretend I had a ball in my arms, and I drove off to the right surrounded by blockers while Kyle ambled to the left, and God bless the Hawley defense because they hated me so much that they followed after me even as I took off *up* the field—in the wrong direction for Pete's sake—and Kyle had only one defender, who he dragged across the goal line.

So now the score was 13–10.

And Red Bend piled all over Kyle and pounded on him while I lay on the field trying to recover from my last tackle, which felt like six elephants instead of three Hawley linesmen who would have been happy to leave me dead, until I finally had to get up just out of simple human pride and join the celebration, and then wait for Beaner's extra point, which of course he made because this was a very special night, and it brought the score up to 14–10, which was even better.

And we won.

And finally they got all the Red Bend players off the field and we all huddled together for a minute on the bench feeling, well, feeling about the way I think I'd feel if I ever tried skydiving and survived it. And then we had to line up and slap hands with the opposition, which is something you have to do after every game. Win even told me once that it was in the Constitution, and I believed him until eighth grade when we studied the Constitution itself and I was surprised to see it wasn't there.

I worked my way down the line, slapping hands like I'd done a thousand times before at basketball and volleyball and summer softball. I could see Brian coming down the line, slapping hands and saying, "Good game," the way you do from the age of six or something on up, up to the pros I guess, and then all of sudden our hands touched and he looked me right in the eye — or I looked him right in the eye if you want to think of it that way—we looked each other in the eye. And he didn't say anything, and neither did I. But I felt, well, I felt a whole book could be written about what we thought, looking at each other. A book with words like Honesty and Trust and Loyalty and Maturity and all those other biggies. I felt like he understood everything I'd been through that night but we would probably never speak again. Not because I was a bad person, or because he was, but because, well, that's just the way the world worked.

And let me say this: of everything that's happened to me this crazy, stupid summer, in that one second that we looked at each other, that's when I felt I grew up the most. And I'll just tell you now, it's not . . . it's not a particularly pleasant sensation.

Brian turned and walked away with his team back to their bus, and Red Bend headed off too, the guys in groups of twos and threes, stopping to cheer with people who'd come onto the field. Beaner had his arm around my shoulders, which was nice except that he kept howling, which made it a little hard to maintain a conversation.

And then in the distance I saw someone and did a double take because she looked so different with her hair brown, and then I took a deep breath and told myself that if I could play a football game I could handle this, and I made my way through the crowd to Amber.

"Hey," I said, coming up beside her, all out of breath.

"Hey. Good game."

"Thanks," I said, so glad she was talking to me. "I didn't think you'd be here."

She shrugged.

The woman next to her, or the girl—sort of between the two, if you know what I mean—shook my hand. "Hey. Amber's told me a lot about you." She had this really cool voice, kind of crackly.

"D.J., this is Dale," Amber explained. "She works in the meat department at the Super Saver."

"Awesome game. You totally rocked out there!"

I shrugged, trying not to make too big a deal out of it and also because I didn't know what to say.

"You know," Dale continued, "we should go partying sometime, the three of us."

"Sure," I said, wondering if the partying would involve Advil. "That'd be fun."

"So . . . we'll see you around?" Amber asked, and I nodded and they ambled away.

I tried with my little beat-up brain to figure out what was different about Amber. Besides the fact that her hair wasn't orange anymore and all. I finally figured it out: she looked happy. I guess I hadn't seen her like that. Ever, really.

And I was happy for her. I really was. But for one thing, I hurt all over. I had a bruise on my thigh that killed me whenever I moved, and my back ached, and I'd done something to my right shoulder during a tackle that made me not want to move my arm too much. But more than that, well, you have to admit it's kind of ironic. I mean, here we are in Nowhere, Wisconsin, and Amber Schneider manages to hook up with someone, someone who actually seems pretty cool and okay. And, well, I don't.

Just then Mom found me to say that there was a reporter looking for me, and even though that would make almost anyone in the world really happy, I knew that if I had to talk to that person the only thing I would do was burst into tears.

"Mommy," I said with all the energy I had, "I just want to go home."

And Mom, God bless her, she understood. She got me over to the Caravan and I stood there stripping off all that goddam gear while Bill and Dad and Aaron shot the breeze like there hadn't even been a seven-month silence between them. Well, not with Aaron, but you get my point. Bill and Aaron had to get back to school right away—Bill had snuck away to see me, which was really great of him, and Aaron had come along because it was his car.

Bill looked over at me at one point. "Jesus, girl, what were you doing all summer?" I guess he was referring to, you know, my muscles and stuff, from all that haying and painting and training and work. Or maybe just to my tan.

Aaron put his arm around my waist. "Damn, Bill. You sure have a good-looking sister."

That part felt nice, if you want to know, his arm around me. I'm big, which I guess you've figured out by now, and my whole family is big. Bill is probably 250 now, and Win's around 215. But Aaron is *big*. It kind of struck me how great it would be to go out with a guy that size. And if you, you know, got tired of dating him, you could always use him as a house or something. So I was happy for a moment, until that little bit of happiness drained away and left me just plain old miserable.

So we all said our goodbyes and Bill and Aaron promised to come to my next game if they possibly could, and Aaron gave me an extra-big squeeze that made me really hope he would, and they left. Curtis had wandered off with a girl somewhere, which normally would be the most amazing thing in the world except I was too bummed out to even care, and Dad took the pickup, so it was just me and Mom.

I stared out the window as Mom worked her way through the parking lot, people waving to us and cheering, and then out on the street. I felt like I'd been playing football for weeks.

"You know what I was thinking about?" Mom asked.

"Mmm," I said, watching the fireflies blink across the fields.

"I was thinking about how hard it must be to play pro ball."

"They earn like two million dollars a year," I couldn't help pointing out.

"I know. But it must be hard being on a team, making all those friends. And then when you're traded, those friends become enemies. You've spent all that time playing with them, learning all their tricks, and then you're expected to go out there and fight them. I think that would be really hard."

I studied her as she drove along, trying to figure out if she was making the point I thought she was making. But she never batted an eye.

"Yeah," I said. "It would be hard." Yeah, I thought to myself. It would almost break your heart.

30

BRIAN NELSON

When I woke up the sun was streaming through the curtains. I panicked for a second about milking and then it all came back to me: the scrimmage, Dad's milking this morning, the touchdown, Bill showing up, Curtis's girlfriend, and then Brian's face when we touched hands after the game. I lay there for a bit just trying to process all this, uneasy because something had woken me up but I couldn't remember what. Then a car door shut — that was it! A car had driven in. That's what woke me. And then I heard, "Hey there, Smut."

Brian.

I leapt out of bed and gave such a scream, because oh my God I hurt all over. If you'd taken me out back and driven the tractor over me you couldn't have done more damage. I sort of staggered and fell on the bed but my butt was sore too, I can't even remember why, and I just had to hold real still and catch my breath for a moment, trying to figure out how to even start moving.

I sat there wriggling my fingers, thinking I'd start slowly, and then the front doorbell rang and it had to be Brian and

I—I'd like to say that it's because I'm a terribly strong and courageous person, but actually I was just too dumb to know better—I grabbed a pair of jeans and headed down the stairs, trying to pull them on as I went down. But I hurt so much I lost my balance halfway down and sort of fell and had to grab the railing for support because my legs didn't work too well and even if they did they were halfway inside the jeans already so I couldn't move them or anything. So instead of walking to the front door I ended up sort of falling against it with a big crash, and I got my jeans zipped up as best I could and took a deep breath and opened the door.

"Hey," I said.

"Hey," said Brian, not looking at me.

The silence lasted about a million years as I tried to pretend I wasn't panting and we both ignored that huge elephant-crashing sound I'd just made, and we both—or I did, anyway, I can't speak for Brian—tried to think of something, anything, anything in the whole wide world, to say.

Plus it didn't help that Smut was exploding with joy to be with both of us.

Brian kicked at the doormat. "I have to talk to you."

"Oh," I said.

Brian looked like he'd rather be anywhere than on our front porch.

Finally I said, because he deserved it, "I'm real sorry."

"About what?" he asked, still not looking at me.

And I realized there were a number of things I could

say. Like about the game—which I wasn't sorry we won, actually—or about what I'd said about his dad, which was just too much to even go into. "I didn't start out wanting to play football. It just sort of happened. And then I didn't tell you . . ." I thought about this for a while, trying to figure out how to explain it, to myself if nothing else. I'd thought about it a lot these past few weeks, trying to figure out what my crazy brain was really up to. "I didn't tell you because I really liked what we had, and I didn't want to screw it up."

Well, that hung there on the front porch for about ten years.

"Jimmy Ott said I had to come here," he said finally, like he hadn't even heard me. "He said I had to thank you."

"Oh," I said. "Don't worry about it. I really liked the training. It was fun."

Brian waved me silent. "Not for that. For the game last night."

"Oh. I didn't mean to, you know, upset you so much."

"Duh. I know that at least." And he couldn't help cracking the tiniest of smiles. But even that smile, microscopic as it was, changed the mood a bit.

So we stood there experiencing that little change of mood. Smut wandered off to find love somewhere else.

"You know what Jimmy said?" Brian said to his shoes. "He said that if I walked off that field, I'd quit like a boy. But if I stayed I'd be playing like a man."

"Wow. That's pretty intense."

"Yeah. I think he practiced it beforehand."

We grinned at that just a bit.

"You were, though," I offered. "At the end, you were someone else."

Brian frowned. "That stuff the Red Bend guys were saying to me —"

"I didn't put them up to that!"

"I know you didn't." He studied his shoes some more. "But it's good you didn't run into me last night."

Just then I heard Dad whistling in the distance. Oh, God, the last person in the world I wanted to see was Dad. Without even thinking I asked, "You want to walk up this way?"

Brian shrugged. But he walked next to me in double time as we circled the house and headed up the hill. We didn't say much for a while, just walked. Smut even caught up to us, carrying her football, hopeful I guess that we'd had brain transplants or something by this point and were all ready to play with her.

It occurred to me that I should say something. I'd spent a lot of time this summer learning how to talk, for the first time really, and now was the time for me to put it to good use. "You know," I said, my voice cracking with fear, "you know, I really missed you these last two weeks."

Brian looked at me. Not studying me or anything like that, but for the first time really looking at me. "I missed you too."

We didn't say anything more. It was pretty weird, walking

the path we'd taken a hundred times up to the heifer field, Smut trotting between us hauling her football, watching us like eventually we'd break down and throw it for her.

"There's this girl," Brian said finally. "Kris. We started going out last summer. She wasn't too happy about me working here, getting all stinked up and everything. She sure doesn't like you."

I listened to this, no idea where it was going, but it just about killed me to hear it.

"I guess she got tired of it, me being so crazy. Like, I kept ragging on you but whenever she said anything about you I'd jump down her throat. Anyway, that's why we broke up." And then to break the tension or something he tossed Smut's football, so I guess she was right in the end, the way she always is.

"How's your arm?" I asked, I guess because that's what you do.

"It hurts. How about you?"

"Oh, I feel great. Just great." We both grinned.

"They really worked you over, didn't they?"

I shrugged.

By this point we were at the heifer field. There were the flags flapping away, and the football field needed a mowing, the lime lines barely visible.

"Dad saw it," I said. I wasn't up for addressing the whole Kris breakup thing.

Brian whistled. "What happened?"

I traced the top of the gate with my finger. "Nothing, I guess." I thought about it some more, how Dad showed up at practice on Thursday, our conversation. I thought about his brownies, and those enormous sandwiches he made for lunch. The way he put cinnamon in French toast. That chicken and prune dish I'd gobbled down that one night that I wouldn't admit was totally delicious. I'd just been too pig-headed to see it before, to notice that my old man was turning into a really good cook. "It was okay, actually. My dad's okay."

Brian looked over the field. "You know what I miss the most? Waiting for you to say something."

"Oh, great."

"Really. When you finally got it out, you always had something to say." All of a sudden he blurted out, "You ever date a football player?"

I thought about going to the movies with Troy Lundstrom. "Not really."

"Me neither," he said, looking off over the trees.

I laughed because it was so funny, but he didn't, and it took me a minute to figure it out. "What? You mean like us?"

He shrugged. "I don't know. It'd be hard, the whole Red Bend–Hawley thing."

"Yeah. Like what do you call it? Romeo and Juliet."

He grinned at me. "I thought you flunked English."

I blushed and then threw the football for Smut just to collect my thoughts. It wasn't that bad a pass either, for me, anyway. "I don't know," I said. "I'd probably end up breaking your arm or something."

Brian laughed. There was this really nice bit of quiet between us.

And right at that moment Mom came puffing up the hill in sweatpants and headphones, looking like she was about to take on Mount Everest. She nodded as she passed like it was the most natural thing in the world for us to run into each other right there in the middle of nowhere. She didn't even slow down.

"What are you doing?" I called out, loudly so she'd hear over her headphones.

"Getting in shape . . . like everyone else . . . in this family," she shouted, heading off over the horizon toward the hay meadow.

We watched her pass.

"Jeez," I said. It was all I could come up with. It was pretty cool, actually, the thought of Mom losing some weight. Maybe now with only one job she really could.

"I should take off," Brian said. But he didn't say it in an I'm Disgusted way. More like an I'll See You Later kind of way.

"Sure," I said. We headed down the hill.

"I told Dad to bag the lawsuit." He sighed. "We'll probably have to talk about that a bunch more."

I considered what he'd just said. "Was this before Jimmy told you to come here, or after?"

"Oh, Jimmy told me that last night. Said I couldn't come back to practice until I'd seen you." Brian grinned at me.

"Wow." I thought about it. "You know, when we were kids Jimmy used to tell us he was our fairy god-uncle. I guess . . . I guess he was right."

Brian smiled to himself. "I guess he was."

We walked all the way back to the Cherokee without saying another word, and then when we got there Brian said, "So, I'll see you around?"

"Yeah. I hope so," I said.

And then because I couldn't figure out anything better I messed up his hair, and then without us even thinking about it he pulled me over and kissed my forehead. And you know what the best part of it was? Neither one of us made a crack about bloody noses. I really appreciated that. I appreciated that a lot.

And he drove away. I stood there and watched him go, Smut sitting next to me, looking back and forth between us like she was waiting for something more to happen. And then after he was gone I scooped up her football and tossed it across the driveway, another pretty good pass for me, and she brought it back, looking all proud the way she always does, and we went inside to see what Dad had made us for lunch.

31

THE END

So now I bet you're wondering what happens, and all I can say is get in line because I'm wondering too. I can't tell you if Red Bend beats Hawley in the big game, and I can't tell you if I end up going out with Brian or even end up friends with him. I can't even tell you if I'm going to be playing football this season, because today is only Labor Day and school starts tomorrow and then they'll make the decision about me playing and all. We're heading out for the Labor Day picnic in a couple minutes, and Dad is downstairs now making a huge racket because he can't find the shredded coconut.

But you know, I think Brian and I will be friends, if we can keep talking. It's pretty weird, us being on different teams and all, but I just have this feeling it'll work out. That was the most amazing part of this summer. Well, meeting Brian and getting to know him was pretty huge. But even more than that, when I really think about it, in terms of life lessons and all, is learning how important it is to keep talking. If you'd asked me back in June what Big Thing I was going to deal with this summer, I sure wouldn't have put that at the top of the list. But when I think about Curtis on that ride back from Madison, or Mom sitting on my bed discussing our family, or that phone call I made to Bill that got him to come see me, or my conversation on the field with Amber and how we're talking again now, or even my complimenting Dad about his cooking . . . all that stuff is important. It really is. It really, really is.

You know, I started writing this thing thinking that it was going to be about football. And describing the scrimmage, and Bill's game two years ago, and all that training I did with Brian, well, that sure covered football enough. But what really surprises me is how much I wrote about other stuff. Because as it turns out — and I'm sure this won't be a revelation to anyone out there with half a brain, even though it was to me — that life isn't all about football.

So anyway, Mrs. Stolze, I hope you like this. It's been pretty amazing, actually, this assignment. When I started two weeks ago I thought I wouldn't have that much to write and that I'd be done in just a couple paragraphs. But it turns out that even if I don't talk a lot, when it's something that matters I still have a lot to say.

Maybe Curtis should try flunking English.

Find out what happens next in D.J.'s life
in the sequel to *Dairy Queen*,
The Off Season

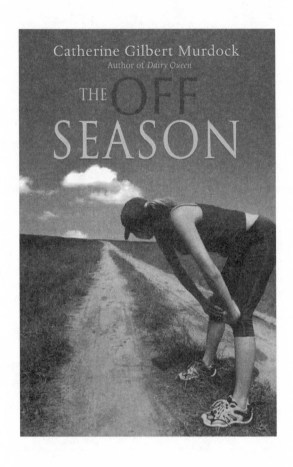

CHAPTER ONE

EVERY LABOR DAY, the Jorgensens — they own Jorgensens' Ice Cream — set up a little ice cream stand right in their yard, which means you can spend the entire Labor Day picnic making yourself ice cream sundaes if that's what you want to do, and for years when I wasn't playing softball or chasing the Jorgensen kids or trying to keep up with my brothers, I'd sit myself at that little booth making one sundae after another until it was time to head home for evening milking, and then a couple miles into the drive I'd bring that whole sundae experience back up, right there on the side of whatever road we happened to make it to. Lately, though, I have a little more self-control. Now I only eat three or four, without marshmallows because I finally figured out that they shouldn't really be part of the whole sundae thing, while I'm hanging out at the pig roast watching guys poke at the fire because apparently it's a law that if you're a guy you have to spend a bunch of time doing that. Then maybe I'll grab one more between innings when I'm not pitching.

That's the other great thing about the picnic: the softball

game. Randy Jorgensen has a huge backyard he mows all year for this, and he borrows bases from Little League so it's official and all. He even got an umpire's getup at a garage sale somewhere, and a friend of his who owns a pig farm works every year as umpire after he's got the pig going in the pit.

My mom used to pitch the game. She pitched all through college, and her team was pretty good from what she's told me. Then one year she threw her back out, which isn't that hard to believe considering she doesn't get much exercise these days and, well, she weighs a whole lot more than she used to. She threw out her back so much that she couldn't walk or anything, Dad had to drive her home in the back of the pickup as she lay there like a piece of plywood if plywood could holler to slow down, and she had to spend three weeks on the living room floor until she healed. Which isn't such a swell thing to be doing when you're supposed to be teaching sixth grade and it's the first three weeks of school.

So she's not allowed to pitch anymore. But at least she started exercising again—not for softball but just to lose some weight—which means puffing around the farm fields, swinging her arms in this way that makes me glad she's not walking where anyone can see her. I guess she figures that an elementary school principal, which she is now since she moved up from teaching sixth grade, shouldn't be quite so heavy.

The softball game is always kids against the grownups,

from little tiny kids still in diapers to old farmers who get their grandkids to run because they don't have any knees left. There's always lots of arguing about where the teenagers should go. This year Randy Jorgensen made a big plea for Curtis, trying to get him on the grownup side on the grounds that he's one of the tallest people there, which is true, but seeing as he's only going into eighth grade he really does belong on the kids' team.

After Mom hurt her back, Randy tried pitching but he took it way too seriously, and the next year Mom suggested me, and now I guess it's just tradition. Which is nice because I don't play school softball seeing as I run track, and this fall of course I was playing football, which is another whole story in and of itself, so this is how I get my softball fix. Plus I'm not too biased. Mom says I'm Switzerland, which I think she means as a compliment.

Besides, it's not like competitive softball. You mostly just try to get the ball across the plate slow enough for whoever's trying to hit it, and keep it dry from the guys who hit with a beer in their other hand. Some little kids hold the bat out like they've never held a bat before, which some of them haven't, and I'll toss the ball as gently as I can against the bat, which in this game counts as a hit, and the kid will be so surprised they'll just stand there while everyone starts hollering, and their mom will have to take them by the hand to run around the bases, and in the meantime the catcher, who's usually

Randy's wife, Cindy, will toss to first but just happen to over-throw, and so the kid will continue on to second just totally amazed, and the second baseman will fumble eight or nine times with a bunch of moaning, and the kid will make it to *third,* and sometimes if there are enough errors the kid will score a home run and walk around on a cloud for the rest of the afternoon.

With other folks, of course, I'm not so nice. Mom always takes a couple turns at bat even though she shouldn't be-cause of her back. All the younger kids in the outfield think this is hilarious, their principal standing there in her big flo-ral shorts and her big pink T-shirt, looking a lot more like a beach ball than a batter. But the older kids know enough to back up. One year she hit the ball so hard it took twenty min-utes to find it. I guess she needs to get her softball fix in too, and also needs to teach those kids a lesson or two about mouthing off.

Then there's Curtis, who's always a huge part of the game, and I'm not just talking about his playing. My little brother might not talk to grownups much, or to me, but with little kids he's just amazing. I don't know if it's because they can tell, the way dogs can sometimes, that he's safe and he'll be really nice to them, which he will. Or maybe he's just a lot more comfortable with kids than older folks, and they pick up on that. But wherever he goes where there are little kids, like this picnic, they just flock to him. As soon as Curtis and this girl he was hanging out with sat down on the edge of the softball field, a half-dozen little kids started climbing on him and giggling and asking him questions, and he settled into it like being a human playground was his calling in life. Whenever the littlest kids went up to bat, he'd run the bases with them if they wanted, and in the outfield he'd make sure they got to tag out their dads and uncles, who often tripped really dramatically right before the base so it'd be easier for the kids to get them.

And then when it was Curtis's turn to hit, the kids got so excited they were just exploding. Curtis after all was a state MVP in Little League, which everyone in town knows including the dead people, and when he walked up to home plate, the kids started zipping like bugs around a porch light, and all the folks in the outfield went *way* back, knowing what was coming, and I switched from nice-girl-tossing-the-ball-against-the-bat to big-sister-you-can-eat-this-one mode.

I pitched a fast one and Curtis swished a strike, and the little kids went bonkers like this was the World Series or something, and then he smashed right through my second pitch and it was clear that all those folks in the outfield hadn't gone back nearly far enough, and he ambled off toward first base because that ball was a couple hours from being found.

A bunch of little kids, though, took that ambling personally. They ran up and started tugging on his arms, and his legs even, shrieking at him to run, and then another bunch of kids, his defenders, decided that this first group shouldn't be so bossy and so they started pulling Curtis the other way because I guess they decided that walking would make him happier. Until finally you couldn't even really see Curtis, just a dozen little kids hollering and waving their arms and giggling hysterically, pulling him in every direction.

You know the expression "fall down laughing"? I actually did. I was laughing so hard, standing there on my little pitcher's mound, that after a while my knees didn't work and I had to lie down and try to breathe as I watched Curtis getting dragged around the bases. It was, hands down, the funniest thing I've ever seen.

Anyway, that's a very long story that doesn't have much to do with anything. But even now that memory makes me grin, Curtis and all those little kids wriggling together . . . It's hard to believe, sitting here in the hospital writing this down, that I ever felt so happy. That once, not so long ago, my life actually seemed okay.